D1145909

COURAGE IN DARKNESS

In an isolated cottage in the Cotswold countryside, a man is typing; at his feet lies an Alsatian, relaxed but watchful. Richard Seal, an ex-naval officer, was blinded in an explosion in the war. A proud and able man, he has fought for his independence. Now he hopes to convey the freedom and excitement of his life at sea in his autobiography. It is into this world of masculine self-sufficiency that Beth comes, sent by an agency to act as his housekeeper. A kind gentle person, Beth has to learn not to impose on his independence or show him pity, while all the time she must conceal her growing feelings of love for him. The second of a trilogy of independent novels of which *Child of Gentle Courage* is the first.

COURAGE IN DARKNESS

SARAH SHEARS

A New Portway Book

CHIVERS PRESS
BATH

First published in Great Britain 1974
by
Elek Books Ltd
This edition published
by
Chivers Press
by arrangement with the author
at the request of
The London & Home Counties Branch
of
The Library Association
1986

ISBN 0 86220 565 4

British Library Cataloguing in Publication Data

Shears, Sarah
Courage in darkness.—(A New Portway book)
I. Title
823′.914[F]   PR6069.H3955

ISBN 0–86220–565–4

Printed and bound in Great Britain by
Redwood Burn Ltd, Trowbridge, Wiltshire

I

In the small porch of the solitary grey-stone cottage, with its thick roof of thatch, Beth Walker, sheltering from the downpour of rain, wiped her streaming face and tucked a wet strand of hair under her hat. She heard a dog growling within the cottage, sensing an intruder, and she was shivering as she lifted the heavy knocker on the oak-panelled door.

It was flung open almost immediately, and she was suddenly confronted by a man and a dog, defensive in their attitude as they stood there, framed in the doorway, waiting for her to speak. The man had the same lean, hungry look as the dog, the same listening face, the same penetrating eyes, the same arrogance. His shaggy brows twitched impatiently, while his hand tightened on the dog's collar. Both the man and the dog, tense with waiting, had caught the gasp of shock and surprise as the door swung open. They knew, instinctively, that whoever was standing there in the porch was afraid and desperately nervous. It gave them both a momentary sense of importance.

'Well?' – the man's voice was harsh.

With a great effort the woman forced herself to speak. 'Good morning. I'm Beth Walker. The Domestic Agency sent me to see you, as I understand you are looking for a daily housekeeper?'

The man's listening face turned to meet her voice, and his sightless eyes held such probing intensity, she was frightened and confused, until he answered with stiff formality.

'Of course, come in, Miss Walker.'

'Mrs,' she corrected quietly.

'Oh, how do you do. I am Richard Seal, and I suppose I should apologise, for I didn't mention the fact I was blind when I phoned the Agency – for obvious reasons!'

The huge dog growled a little as the woman followed them over the threshold, and the man laughed harshly.

'Sheba doesn't seem to approve, but sometimes she objects to sharing me with people. I hope you like dogs, Mrs Walker? You won't be much use to me if you don't!'

He spoke with the voice of one given to authority, as indeed he was.

'I have a dog of my own, though nothing like the size of Sheba. Mine's a spaniel,' she told him quietly.

'Good! Then I expect Sheba will accept you – eventually. Give her time. Sit over there, near the fire, then we can talk.'

She sat down awkwardly on the edge of an old-fashioned, high-backed chair; her wet coat clinging to her sturdy figure, her gloved hands clasped tightly in a desperate attempt to still their trembling. She felt the penetrating stare of those dark eyes, and found herself hastily pushing more wet strands of hair into place, and wishing she had worn her best shoes. But Richard Seal asked none of the usual questions, and the interview was unlike any other.

'I want someone who will not object to leaving the housework from time to time, to read over a few pages of typescript and make corrections. I'm writing a book,' he explained. 'I had the phone installed to cut down on the correspondence, but I get the odd letter, of course. Thanks to St Dunstan's thorough training, I'm practically independent, but not self-sufficient! Sheba is my better half. We have a perfect understanding.'

His hand caressed the stiff pointed ears, and the dog's adoring eyes searched the man's face, waiting for the tender smile that played about his hard mouth.

'I can manage breakfast and supper myself,' he continued,

'but I like a cooked meal at midday – anything, I'm not fussy about food. The rest is entirely up to you. Could you come from ten till three, six days a week? You could leave me something to warm up at the weekends. I can offer you five pounds, with dinner, of course. You may be worth more; I daresay you are, but that's my limit,' he added quite positively. 'I know it looks pretty grim at the moment, but it shouldn't take long to get it ship-shape. The last housekeeper packed up a week ago, but she was pretty hopeless – left every darn thing lying around in all the wrong places. Sheba couldn't stand her! She's an aloof sort of creature at the best of times, but that woman couldn't get anywhere near her.'

Beth Walker had already decided that her predecessor was a poor thing, anyway, for it was all too apparent the place had been sadly neglected. It was dreary and dusty; the brasses unpolished and the windows coated with accumulated damp and dust. Beyond in the kitchen she could see the table and the sink piled with dirty dishes.

'Don't let those dirty dishes put you off, Mrs Walker. When I've nothing left to use, I shall wash up!'

She blushed unwittingly, for he had guessed her thoughts.

'Well, that's about all, I think. Are you interested in the job? You haven't said a word yet,' he complained.

'I was waiting for you to finish,' she reminded him, in that calm, quiet voice he found so soothing.

It would be good for them to have someone calm and quiet about the place, Richard thought, still fondling the dog's head.

'Would you like to try it for a month?' he persisted.

'Thank you, yes, I should,' she answered without hesitation.

But it still rankled that she was doing it out of pity and for no other reason, and he wanted to shout at her 'don't pity me, woman, for God's sake!' Instead, because he had to be finished with this baffling business of interviewing prospective housekeepers, he kept his mouth shut.

'I think I should explain about myself, after all, I'm a total stranger?' she suggested, tentatively.

He shrugged. What difference could it make? Sheba was obviously satisfied, so that was the most important factor in the engagement.

'I have a cottage in the village, bequeathed by an aunt at the end of the war. I make it my base, and spend about three months of the year there. The rest of the time I spend in other people's houses as an emergency housekeeper. I take my dog with me,' she added. 'The Agency have my references, Mr Seal, if you will phone them for confirmation?'

He listened with scant attention. He was not interested in references, but he realised now he had made a mistake in telling the Agency it was an emergency. He was frowning, and cursing himself for a fool when she answered his unspoken question.

'There is no limit to the engagement, Mr Seal; I stay as long as I am needed.'

He sighed with relief and grinned.

'Well, that's fine, you had me worried for a moment! When can you start?' he demanded.

'Now, if you wish?'

He was still grinning. 'You will? – splendid! Thanks!'

He pulled the dog's ears playfully, and Sheba banged her tail on the floor.

Beth Walker looked them over with pride and satisfaction – her new employers! She wondered how long it had taken Richard Seal to acquire such an immaculate appearance? How many months of clumsy, impatient fumbling would straighten a blinded man's tie? How many frustrated hours before he could feel a crease in his trousers, and know that his shoes were polished like a mirror? His thick greying hair was smooth and well-trimmed; but how did he manage to shave himself?

Her lips trembled, not with pity – her admiration took

away all the pity – but because she could see him, in her mind's eye, when he was learning to do all these things for himself at St Dunstan's. Sheba too was well-groomed, and her coat shone with vigorous brushing. She was alert and healthy. Her black nose was damp, and her lolling tongue showed fine strong teeth.

But Richard Seal's face bore the lines of mental conflict, and his brows twitched nervously. When he had grinned, she had caught a fleeting glimpse of the man he used to be, before he was struck by blindness. He had told her briefly, 'I'm a Naval man, I was blinded in October, 1944. We were on convoy in mid-Atlantic, when we ran into a German U-boat. It was pretty grim.' That was all. She didn't expect him to go into any more details, but he had told her enough to imagine the horror and the tragedy of that ghastly experience.

'Well, now we've got that settled, I'll make you a cup of coffee,' he was saying.

'Let me do it, please!' she urged.

He shrugged and warned, 'Don't start spoiling me!'

'I won't!'

She was smiling confidently now, as she went past him towards the kitchen, and was no longer afraid of the man or the dog. But her wet coat had been steaming beside the fire, and he demanded, frowningly, 'Why didn't you say you were soaking wet?'

'It's nothing. Rain doesn't bother me, I'm used to it. I've lived in the Cotswolds most of my life. How do you like your coffee?'

'Black and strong!'

He heard her busy in the kitchen, and soon the fragrant aroma drifted through to him. His acute hearing detected a slight hesitation in the handling of the cups on the tray when she poured the coffee.

'Just put it down here and I can reach for it,' he told her, 'and two spoons of sugar. By the way, a letter came this morning. You might just open it and read it when you've had your coffee.'

He walked across to the desk, passed a practised hand along the row of pigeon holes, and took out an envelope.

'There's a paper knife somewhere.'

Again his hand spread over the tidy desk, and closed on the ivory handle.

Beth slit the flap and read aloud.

> 'Dear Sir,
>
> I received your message from the landlord of the Crown last week, and I write to inform you I shall be free to start on the patching job on your thatched roof about the middle of next month. In the meantime, I should advise a large tarpaulin over the leaking patch. They would lend you one at Cowley Farm.
>
> Yours faithfully,
>
> Tom Little
>
> P.S. We always get a lot of rain this month, so I should get the roof covered quickly.'

'Blast! I expected him this week. These thatching chaps are getting mighty independent,' Richard complained testily.

'He's probably busy on stacks at this time of the year, and Tom Little is one of the few expert thatchers left in this part of the country,' Beth reminded him. 'He's a real artist, and I've often watched him at work on one of the old cottages in the village. He was very disappointed, I remember, that not one of his three sons would carry on with the craft. It's sad in a way to see all these old country crafts dying out.'

Richard said he supposed so, but he still felt only irritation for further delay.

'Is it a big leak?' asked his new housekeeper anxiously.

'Bad enough to need a bucket to catch the drips!'

She gasped and hurried upstairs.

'Yes, there is a big wet patch on the ceiling, and it seems to be spreading,' she told him, rather breathlessly, when she came back.

'I could have told you that!' he reminded her. 'Well, I must phone the farm and get that tarpaulin sent round, and then I must get some work done.'

Feeling dismissed, Beth went back to the kitchen, and started to clear the stack of dirty dishes. An old-fashioned boiler provided plenty of hot water, and a small back scullery had been converted into a bathroom. Through the kitchen window she could see a neglected garden, and beyond the hedge, open fields.

The rain was sweeping across the grey sky, and the last of the leaves swirled and danced in the wind. But Beth was neither dismayed nor depressed by the bleak landscape, for she was a part of it, and it suited her nature. She was not one of those women who craved for holidays in the sun, and who rushed off to Spain and Italy every Summer. Rain and wind were her natural elements, and she thrived on hardship. She was middle-aged now and grey-haired, but had not seen a doctor since the end of the war. Then it had not concerned her health, but a broken leg – and shock.

Jimmy had been killed when the car overturned after hitting the side of the lorry on a sharp bend. He was never a very careful driver. It was their first holiday together, and they were on their way to Scotland. Twenty years a widow! A sad little smile flitted across her weathered face, and her soft, brown eyes held memories of another world. So long ago, it seemed sometimes that she had never known marriage, or a man's love and companionship. It was animals, not people, she loved so passionately now, and Cindy was her constant companion.

Sheba would be a one-man dog and hardly notice her, for she had been specially trained for one blinded man or woman.

Beth was glad to be working again in a home where an animal played so important a part. Once again she knew she was going to be happy, because their need of her was urgent, and her sense of dedication satisfied. It was not enough to have a job and a wage at the end of the week. She had to feel she was useful and absolutely necessary. The old and the young had claimed her, used her, and let her go. She stayed only until her services were obviously superfluous, then she packed her bag and left. It was her life.

So she tied on the grubby apron left behind by her predecessor – tomorrow she would wear a pretty nylon overall – and washed the dishes with easy and accustomed hands. Methodically she planned the remainder of the day, and the dinner she could provide from the scanty bits and pieces in the larder. Today it would have to be a make-shift meal, but tomorrow she would get properly organised!

She wondered what Richard Seal was writing about so industriously. He seemed to be an expert typist, judging from the speed. Yet another of the accomplishments for which he had to thank St Dunstan's, she supposed? Sheba lay at his feet, with her head on her paws, but alert to every sound and movement. It was, she thought, the most wonderful relationship she had ever seen between a human and canine creature. They seemed to be completely absorbed in one another, to the exclusion of any other person.

Three hours later, when she had cleaned the four small rooms, and seen Richard Seal eat, sparingly, of a cottage pie and tinned pears, Beth remembered he had not bothered to phone the Agency to check on her credentials. Perhaps he intended to do so after she left, but he seemed to have taken her on trust? Sheba, too, had accepted her, and allowed her to move about the cottage freely, watching her pass with roving, limpid eyes.

She was filling the coal buckets rather noisily in the coal

shed, when she heard Richard Seal call sharply and authoritatively . . .

'Leave that! It's my job.'

Surprised by the harshness of his voice, she dropped the shovel and went indoors.

'I'm sorry,' she said simply, as she went through to the kitchen to hang up the apron on the pantry door. She was tired now, and flushed with exertion. Strands of soft hair hung in wisps about her face. It was time for a cup of tea. From the kitchen door she looked directly at Richard Seal, sitting at his typewriter, but no longer absorbed and busy. The waste-paper basket was spilling over with screwed balls of paper. His face was strained and pale, his mouth twitching.

'Damn it!' he exploded. 'I've still got two good hands! I'm not helpless!'

'I said I was sorry,' she reminded him quietly, her throat contracting, her eyes smarting with tears. Would she ever get used to his sudden bursts of temper, and violent moods? Should she know instinctively all the things he could do for himself, and wanted to, so desperately?

'I was going to make a cup of tea?' she suggested.

'Not for me, thanks, I need something stronger.'

He pushed back his chair, went to the sideboard, and poured himself a double whisky with practised self-assurance.

As she drank a cup of tea, she asked tentatively, 'Would you like me to read the typescript before I go? Or haven't you finished your quota for today?'

'Finished? I wish to God I had never started!' he retorted. 'An author – me?' he laughed mirthlessly. 'I should have stuck to shopkeeping, at least I knew the routine, and the customers were decent. Nobody ever tried to cheat me in all the ten years I had my own business. But I got so bored and fed up selling packets of cigarettes and boxes of matches. It was too easy, too automatic, I was getting to be a robot, getting stale. So I went back to St Dunstan's and took a typewriting course. When I told them to find me an isolated cottage where I could write a book in peace, they thought I wanted my brains tested. They were right! Blast them!'

His tortured face and dark, compelling eyes frightened her again. Immediately, sensing her fear, his face became strangely still and controlled.

'I beg your pardon,' he said in a taut voice. 'Now, will you please go.'

She went out without a word, closing the door softly.

For a long time he sat slumped in the chair, with the dog's head between his knees. The rain had stopped and Sheba was whimpering to go out.

'Why can't I keep my blasted mouth shut?' he asked her, savagely. 'Now we have seen the last of Mrs Walker, and she was doing pretty well. I guess you are the only one who can put up with me now, Sheba. God! I feel awful! My head! Come on, let's get out of here. We both need fresh air and exercise.'

They went out together, the huge, powerful dog, and the tall, lean man. Sheba was wearing her white harness, and at the bottom of the narrow lane the dog pulled up sharply, and they both climbed easily over the high stile. Side by side in the open field they stood, pressed close together, their dark intent faces lifted to the clean, cold, tingling wind. Then, wheeling suddenly, they began to pace a certain well-trod path in long, prowling strides. Alert to every sound and every change of weather, Richard felt the wind veer round to south-west.

'He was right, that thatcher fellow, confound him! More rain on the way,' he told Sheba.

The rough path under his feet bore no resemblance to the well-scrubbed decks of his youth and early manhood, but his thoughts had wings. The pacing of the narrow path across the stubbly field measured exactly the length of the boat deck on his last ship. With his dog close to him, and nothing between them and the stormy sky, his taut muscles slackened, and all his harshness melted away.

When Richard got back to the cottage that evening and made a careful tour, he discovered, to his intense relief, that everything was ship-shape. The faint odour of floor polish still lingered when he opened the door, but he went through to the kitchen to prepare supper, and found the stove free of grease, and the saucepans stacked in a neat row overhead, with all the handles facing the same way. All the dirty dishes had disappeared, and the table left entirely clear. Cups were back on their hooks, and plates and saucers in neat piles on the shelf. The tea caddy had been put back on the window sill. Everything, in fact, was exactly where he expected to find it, but so seldom did, with the last housekeeper. She seemed a sensible sort of woman, he told Sheba, and a pity he lost his temper about the coal buckets. People simply would not realise he was a normal man – apart from his blindness – and what normal man would allow a woman to fill up and carry heavy coal buckets?

Nevertheless, if she turned up in the morning – which he very much doubted, after the way she had been treated on her first day – they must both try very hard to please her, he reminded the dog. Women put great value on small unimportant details, such as wiping the mud off your feet on the doormat, putting the cigarette ends in the ash trays, and folding your pyjamas! But, apart from all that, they must keep their tempers under control, and remember to be tolerant of a sighted person's many idiosyncrasies!

Sheba listened carefully, her paws leaving their wet impression on the freshly scrubbed kitchen floor. She waited, with the patience born of long experience and intuition of his blindness, for the meat to be cut into small chunks and mixed with hard biscuits from the top shelf of the larder.

'Take a look at that, you bullying bitch!' the man

demanded, playfully slapping the bowl on the floor. 'And watch out you don't spill it on the floor! I can smell it's clean.'

This was the hour of the day the dog loved best, after their evening patrol in the field, when they came back to supper. The close bond that bound them together in their need of each other, held, during the long busy day, a sense of urgency, and a driving, relentless purpose. They were constantly alert and aware of the rest of the world. In their mutual regard for each other, they had become so acutely sensitive, one could not be aware of danger, or anger, or fear, or pleasure, or pain, without the other. But, with the coming of nightfall, they were withdrawn and safe – relaxed and relieved that another working day had passed.

'Now, Sheba, we can let our hair down!' Richard would say, and they would both stretch and yawn luxuriously.

While the dog ate her supper, the man was busily preparing his own, and his hands were deft and sure, without fumbling or groping. The huge dog with her hunger appeased, sat back on her haunches, watching every familiar movement, with mingled pride and pleasure. Her body was quivering now with the eager anticipation of sampling the food the man was preparing with such delicate and precise care.

On this particular evening, it was sausages, bacon and fried potatoes, for Richard was famished. When he sat down at the table, with the appetising smell drifting through the cottage, he remarked casually 'Smells good!' and cut a sausage neatly in half. Sheba's tail quivered on the kitchen floor, and she sucked in her tongue expectantly, opening and closing her jaws. But she did not move an inch. She stayed exactly one pace away from the table, disciplined and obedient. Her behaviour was always a copy of the man's, and since Richard neither sprawled nor spread his arms at the table, but sat erect, with a clean table napkin spread over his knees, the dog's behaviour was equally admirable. An arm reached out, with the half sausage suspended on a fork, and Sheba bent her proud head to take it, very gently and politely, swallowed it whole, licked her jaws, and waited for the next tit-bit.

'I'll make some coffee,' Richard told her later, and then she knew for certain the meal was over.

With the supper dishes washed and carefully put away in all the right places, they went back to the sitting-room, with the pot of coffee, and Richard settled comfortably in the big arm-chair, and lit a cigarette. The dog lay with her head on the man's knees, searching the stern, familiar face with tender eyes.

Some time later, a hand ran expertly over the dial of the braille watch, then moved across to the radio to turn a knob. 'The Navy Lark,' he told Sheba, stretching his long legs to the blazing fire. Then his grim mouth relaxed into a smile of pleasant anticipation.

The radio was an indispensable necessity to Richard Seal, for it kept him informed of the world he once knew. The regular news bulletins were milestones in his busy day, and the evening entertainment, chosen discriminately, provided all that he needed for relaxation and pleasure. At least he was trying to convince himself it was sufficient, but it was taking a hell of a long time!

It was nearly two years already since the divorce, two years of tormenting memories and self-reproach, for he knew he was to blame. To live without a woman and without love was taking a heavy toll of his disciplined nerves and senses. Every day now he lost control over some trivial incident or slight frustration, and then he was ashamed. It would be excusable, he argued, in a younger man, new to blindness, but he was middle-aged and had lived in a world of darkness for twenty years. How could he honestly pretend these years had been happy years, for Marion or himself? They had both been shattered by the cruel fate which had deprived him of sight, only six months after their marriage, when their young inexperienced love had not been strong enough to hold together the crumbling resources of their changed lives.

When, at last, Richard returned from St Dunstan's, trained, disciplined and independent, he was a stranger to his young wife – a stranger in every sense of the word. Gentleness had turned to arrogance; sweetness to bitterness; trust to suspicion. The flat that once had seemed so big and spacious, now seemed cramped. Invariably it overflowed with Marion's theatrical friends from the local repertory company. She had become quite an accomplished actress, and was actually playing the lead in a new production when he arrived back, to spoil her happiness by his jealous possessiveness. The more she eluded him, the more he craved for her company, and a return to the old enchantment of their brief courtship. But it was impossible to recapture the love they had known. It belonged to another age, another couple. They had both matured beyond all recognition.

So they went their separate ways – she to the theatre, and he to the little tobacconist shop; with a white stick clearing the traffic from his path. He was too proud to ask help from anyone.

During the winter of 1958, Marion went on tour to Australia for six months, and Richard, who had previously applied for a guide dog, left the shop in charge of his young assistant, and spent a month at a guide dog training centre. It was here he met Sheba and they were instantly attracted to one another. It was a wonderful experience to feel the dog responding to his voice, his touch, and his sensitive handling. At the end of the month's training, when they encountered every type of traffic problem – or so it seemed to Richard – he returned home with Sheba. He put away his white stick with a sense of freedom and independence he had not known since he left St Dunstan's.

Proudly he walked with Sheba along the familiar pavements and across the busy streets. There was a new purpose in his bold stride and a new awareness in his shadowed face. It was a new kind of loving and loyalty he had not known existed between a canine and a human creature.

They were quite inseparable, for Sheba slept at the side of his bed. But his strong, virile body was starved and restless, and his sleep often disturbed by tantalising visions of Marion. She would be ageless, this woman, and forever young and beautiful. That was the mockery of his blindness. He saw her only with the eyes of his young and ardent youth, and not through the eyes of today.

2

For the second day Beth Walker stood hesitating in the front porch of Rose Cottage, wondering what lay beyond that solid oak-carved door. But today she would not lift the heavy knocker, or leave her bicycle propped against the fence. She would push it round to the wood shed, and enter by the back door. She was hesitating to get her breath back after the two mile ride in a boisterous wind, and she remembered Richard Seal had not asked her how she got there in yesterday's deluge, though he must realise, surely, his cottage was isolated? She supposed he travelled by taxi, and people who used any form of mechanical transport seldom had any idea of distance, or regard for cyclists and pedestrians!

She was feeling a little apprehensive about starting on this new job, after yesterday's alarming initiation! But the challenge it presented would be good for her, she argued, from the safety of the front porch, and it would take more than the combined forces of a masterful man and his dog to dislodge her from the task she had accepted. She was gentle but not weak! But she knew this was no ordinary routine job, and unlike any other she had undertaken in the past two decades. It would need all her patience and tolerance, test her courage, and hurt her feelings. She would have to defend herself against his harsh laugh and black moods – with silence and a quiet withdrawal.

Yesterday had shown her the only way to combat these sudden inexplicable rages. He would never know she was acutely sensitive, and how she trembled at a harsh word. It was a constant battle she had fought since childhood, and quietness covered her cowardice. She was desperately afraid of all things violent, harsh and cruel. Beneath the calm surface of her gentleness and soft brown eyes, she wrestled with this super-sensitiveness, for it spoiled her enjoyment of life. She knew she wore humility like a mask, as Richard Seal wore a mask of arrogance. She would probably never know the real man, and he would not know the real woman.

Jimmy had not known the real woman behind the gentle mask – a woman so desperately eager to love and be loved, yet so afraid. There had been no time, no opportunity, in their hurried courtship and marriage on the shore leave provided so unexpectedly during the last year of war. Torn with remorse, after his sudden and violent death, Beth remembered only his charm and gaiety, and his rich enjoyment of life. Given time and understanding, it could have been such a happy marriage – she told herself repeatedly. But they had no time and Jimmy was, perhaps, too young and impatient.

Why did she remember him so vividly now, on the threshold of another chapter? She must pull herself together, and show a brave front, for this man, with his sightless eyes could see more than the other. She already knew it would be difficult to escape the frightening compulsion of those dark staring eyes, for in some mysterious way they held a probing intensity beyond the realms of sight. This man, who had engaged her for the purpose of cleaning his home, cooking his meal, and reading the pages of typescript his fertile brain had created, would use her, as the others had used her. He might even exploit her usefulness, for his need was greater, and she was easily exploited. But he would also drain the struggling resources of equanimity and assurance she had built around her natural timidity in self-defence. She thought he would be utterly self-absorbed – self and Sheba.

For Richard Seal, she would be just another housekeeper

and a useful commodity, on which to throw all the irritating frustrations of his ambitions as an author. As for Sheba, she might treat the female intruder with proud disdain. There would be none of the friendly familiarity of the other dogs in the other homes. Sheba, so rightly named, would be a queen among dogs, and one did not trifle with the friendship of a queen!

For her own comfort and companionship she would still have Cindy, the gentle little spaniel with the soft pleading eyes and clinging paws. She had made a surprising discovery last night, when she saw their two faces reflected in the mirror. They had both developed the same expression – it was quite extraordinary. Or was it? She remembered when the door of Rose Cottage swung open, and her gasp of astonishment, for the man and the dog had a frightening similarity – the same proud tilt of the head, the same grim expression, the same arrogance. Did people grow like their pets, or pets like people? It was an interesting reflection. But Cindy had been puzzled by the change of routine, and a little unhappy to be left alone in the cottage. A neighbour's child had promised to take her for a walk in the school dinner hour. Fortunately they were right in the middle of the High Street and not isolated. Anyone who heard her whining would go in to comfort her. Everyone in the village knew Cindy.

The hammer of the typewriter keys drowned her tentative tap on the back door, but Sheba growled and the tapping stopped.

'Come in!' called Richard Seal.

Beth took a deep breath, pushed open the door and went inside.

'Good morning, Mrs Walker!'

They were standing, side by side, in front of the big desk, and again she noticed the striking resemblance between the man and the dog. But today they had mellowed, and they were obviously intending to be different! They both wore a look of pleading penitence that disturbed her almost as much as the proud arrogance of the previous day. It seemed so forced and unnatural, as though they had been rehearsing the scene for her benefit.

'Good morning,' she answered chokingly.

Sheba had one paw raised, and Richard Seal explained. 'Sheba wants to shake hands with you, Mrs Walker.'

So Beth stepped forward and obligingly shook the dog's paw. It was, in itself, an act of contrition for yesterday's behaviour, and served both as an apology and a truce. She could understand such a gesture, for it had dignity and restraint. She hadn't expected a profuse apology from this man, but he was going to be even more unpredictable than she had anticipated. His moods, apparently, ranged from playful to poisonous, and she must learn to live with them, from ten till three. She was glad, though, he hadn't asked her to be a resident housekeeper, for the nervous tension that surrounded them was almost electric!

Now she looked them over, once again, with pride and pleasure, for they both were shiningly clean and well-groomed. There was no muddle or litter in the small sitting-room, and beyond in the kitchen, the breakfast dishes were neatly piled on the draining board. The coal scuttles had been filled and a pile of small logs stacked in the corner of the big old-fashioned fender.

'It all looks very ship-shape,' said Beth brightly.

Richard raised his eyebrows inquiringly. 'Ship-shape? That's a nautical term you don't often hear from a land-lubber.'

'Is it?' she parried, a deep flush flooding her cheeks.

'Have any of your jobs taken you overseas?'

'One – years ago.'

'East or West?'

'East.'

'Ah, the fascination of the Orient! We must talk about it some time,' he said, vaguely. Then he changed the subject.

In the pink nylon overall she looked clean and efficient. Yesterday she had felt like a charwoman in the grubby apron. Today she felt like a housekeeper again. She, too, had her pride!

'Would you mind leaving this room till last, Mrs Walker? I seem to be making quite good progress with chapter ten this morning, and it would be a pity to waste the trend of thought!' He grinned, affably.

'Of course, I'll do it any way you like. It makes no difference to me – but I like to be called Beth,' she told him, quietly. He looked pleased.

His mobile face seemed to have registered the whole range of emotions, already, in the few short hours she had known him.

'I don't want to be awkward, but to me this is important. I've got to get it out of my system,' he explained.

'I understand. What are you calling your book?'

'The Sea was my Mistress.'

'Rather an intriguing title. Have you found a publisher, or does that come later?'

'I've found one prepared to consider it. A chap I knew at St Dunstan's gave me an introduction last Summer. I spend all my holidays at Ovingdean. It's my second home!' he laughed.

'You haven't any family, then?'

'No – I spent my childhood in a Children's Home. What you never have, you never miss, they say. It was the only home I remember, anyway, for I was orphaned before I was three years old. Well – enough of that! I must get back to work. Would you make me a pot of coffee – black and strong – and put it over here, then I can help myself.'

'Before you start, could we just settle the question of meals and supplies?' Beth reminded him, quickly. 'There was nothing much in the larder yesterday, so I took the liberty of buying a couple of pork chops, some vegetables and apples for a pie. Is that all right?'

'Very sensible! Buy anything you like, I leave it to you. The butcher calls on Tuesdays and Saturdays, the baker on Monday and Thursday, the grocer only once a week – Friday as a rule. Remind me about it again before you go, then we can make out the weekly order and you can phone it through. How much did you spend today?'

'Eight and tenpence.'

'Right.'

He took a handful of coins from his pocket and counted out the exact amount on to the table.

'That's settled.'

Then he waited for the coffee with an anxious little frown puckering his eyes. His long, sensitive hands lay motionless on his knees. Suddenly the keys began to rattle, and Sheba settled down to her long vigil.

Beth went back to the kitchen and softly closed the door. Richard Seal had already withdrawn into his private world, and she was dismissed.

It was one of those nights of nervous tension, when sleep was as far removed as the moon. A desperate longing for the woman he still loved became a hunger in the long, lonely hours before dawn. Sheba's warm, wet tongue on his outflung hands was comforting, but it was not enough. Richard fondled the dog's ears absentmindedly, and remembered again, in every vivid detail, the day he had learned the truth about Marion; when all the years of discord and disharmony had finally collapsed. There was nothing he could do about these nights of tortured memories, only to let each memory pass across his mind as a picture on a screen. The suffering it brought was, in a way, self-inflicted, but he endured it, as a man would endure a flogging, because to spare himself was to become a weakling and a coward. He drove himself relentlessly, and fought the easy claims of self-indulgence. It was almost an obsession now, and he watched his weight as carefully as he watched the hours he must spend in working out the formula of his book. He couldn't bear to feel sluggish, mentally or physically. Mind and body must grow, develop and mature throughout life, he reasoned. There was no limit to his endurance, no boundary beyond the world of blindness he could not reach, he reminded himself, repeatedly.

Peace of mind was no substitute for the crowding ambitions and the wide scope of opportunities he knew existed, even for a man without sight.

He wished, now, he had not been persuaded into shopkeeping in the early years of blindness, but it was Marion's suggestion, and Marion he wanted to please. But she hadn't intended to be a shopkeeper's wife, only to get him standing, firmly and squarely, on his own two feet! The clever little bitch!

It was during these tortured nights of memory when he remembered the day, even the exact moment, the shattering ultimatum reached him.

He was sitting in the sun lounge at Ovingdean, smoking a cigarette and listening, in a vague, amused way, to one of the afternoon visitors reading out notices of West End shows, actors and actresses, film stars, pop singers, and such like, and several of the new chaps, including young Jackson, recently blinded, seemed thirsty for such information.

'Here's a picture of Marion Sherwood, leaving London Airport with her leading man, Clive Baker,' the voice announced to his young audience.

Young Jackson remarked, innocently, 'A smashing couple! I've seen all their shows. Aren't they husband and wife in private life?'

The visitor laughed. 'Unofficially, I believe. But she is still tied up to one of your chaps. Didn't you know? He must be somewhere in his mid-forties now, but then she's no chicken, either!'

'Gosh!' breathed young Jackson, excitedly. 'My ears are flapping, tell me more.'

Richard Seal had struggled out of the deep armchair and walked out, with a blank face, holding the dog's collar.

He ran into Matron in the corridor.

'Hello, Richard – are you feeling all right?'

'Yes, I'm okay, thanks.'

But he was deathly pale, and his twitching mouth betrayed him. Matron was always the soul of diplomacy, and fussing over a man like Richard Seal would only tend to make matters worse.

'Won't you join me in a cup of tea? I've just made a pot in my sitting-room,' she asked, in that brisk, matter-of-fact voice he had grown to like and trust in the early months of training. It had been the first voice he had liked, when blindness had left him so dependent on voices. Other voices had been shocked, pitying, apprehensive, and just plain stupid! But at Ovingdean he met normality, and responded immediately to its bracing elements.

After a few moments he seemed more relaxed, and a faint tinge of colour crept back into his pallid cheeks. She watched him with the kindly eyes of one who has grown familiar with blindness, yet never grown critical. She was one of the few people who agreed with Richard that the boundaries beyond the world of blindness held few limitations, and her encouragement was wise and practical. Looking now at the middle-aged Richard Seal, with the greying hair, she remembered the young Richard, and smiled nostalgically, for she had liked and admired him tremendously for all his arrogance and vile temper! At least he was alive!

Some were too shocked and stunned, or too drowned in

self-pity to be interested in anything or anybody. Some were so apathetic they groped their way around with faces as blank as masks. Some refused to accept blindness and were devastated by the specialist's ultimatum.

But Richard Seal had the courage that was needed to face the truth. There was, for him, no hope at all of ever regaining sight. He had asked for the truth and got it. Like so many young naval men, Richard had grown a beard. Shaving was one of the early accomplishments to master in a world without sight, and the beard came off in the early days at Ovingdean. Others had admired the courage of the new young trainee, and been amused by his arrogance and dominant personality.

Blindness had not changed his natural instinctive leadership. He was not an easy person to train because he found it more difficult than many of his contemporaries to master what Matron called the three 'Ps' – Patience, Persistence, Perspective. She thought he must surely have been one of the most impatient young men who ever set foot in St Dunstan's! Richard had expected to learn braille in a couple of weeks, and to find his way around the house and grounds while others were too frightened to move.

No, one did not easily forget such an alarming person as young Richard Seal, Matron decided.

He still had the same distinguished good looks, and his dark, magnetic eyes still shone in his lean face with the brightness of onyx. He was evidently not intending to confide in her, at the moment, but she knew, by long experience, he had received a severe shock of some kind. His sensitive face could still register every emotion, but when he pleased he pulled a shutter down, and hid behind its blankness. In a way, she supposed he was still very much the lone wolf at Ovingdean, for since he had been trained with a guide dog, he had become even more independent. She had been the first to see the striking resemblance in the dog and the man, when they first came to Ovingdean together for a Summer holiday. With a towel slung over his shoulder, Richard would stride the tunnel which connected the grounds to the beach, whistling shrilly. Sheba was a little more reluctant to leave the safety of dry land, but her doubts were lost in her obvious duty to this man who demanded so much of her canine courage. She met the advancing waves with shivers of fear, but the man plunged in boldly, with a rich throaty shout. It was the voice of triumph and the voice of authority.

'Come on in, Sheba! Come on! It's marvellous!'

So Sheba, frightened and appalled by the strength of the sea, fought gamely to endure it, for his sake. Whatever happened, she knew, instinctively, she must never let him out of her sight.

'Come on! Where are you? Sheba! Come on!'

As one of the 'old boys' of Ovingdean, he was still entitled to go back for holidays, or any refresher course of training helpful to his career or livelihood. Because Richard Seal's actress wife, Marion Sherwood, had been almost constantly engaged with rehearsals, shows and tours since their marriage, they had seen a lot of him, and he usually turned up twice a year and spent Christmas with them. The Commandant welcomed this particular 'old boy' with warm enthusiasm, for he brought such an air of assurance and independence, it was, in itself, an advertisement for the place, he told Matron. And Matron agreed that Richard Seal, at middle age, was still a shining example of a skilled and disciplined St Dunstaner.

He would go on a tour of inspection with Sheba, meeting several of the old instructors and teachers he had known as a young man. To the new trainees he was a miracle man, for he had not only achieved independence, but had also possessed an actress wife! This, they felt, was something much more remarkable than winning awards and diplomas!

Some were struggling with the intricacies of weaving on

the looms in the workshop, and Richard recalled his own frustrating attempts to make a scarf.

'I shall never get the hang of this blasted thing!' he had exploded, during the first lesson. Afterwards he had felt ashamed when others were in the same state, but keeping their mouths shut. It had been the same with the basket and rug-making, sewing on buttons and darning socks. It was all so tedious and laborious he nearly went mad. But it was all part of the training, and the long road to independence. The only alternative was to walk out, and be led by the hand for the rest of his life. This appalling prospect made even rug-making bearable. But even blindness had its compensations, and he soon discovered he was an apt pupil in the gymnasium. Sports Day always found him as a competitor in the field events, the gymnast display, and all the swimming and rowing events. With long, concentrated practice, he acquired a fair amount of skill at the firing range, but was always beaten by a chap called Sparks Harris, his biggest rival.

All this led up, eventually, to that inevitable day, which everyone had foreseen, when he found himself in Matron's office, with Sheba, and the devastating ultimatum he now had to face.

It was the one obvious fact he could not accept – the one reality he would not recognise. In everything else he was a realist, and he was undaunted. But in everyone there is a weakness and a flaw, and Richard was no exception. Stubbornly, he clung to the illusion of a better understanding with Marion, as a drowning man clings to a life-belt. Because he still loved her, he refused to believe the quarrels and misunderstandings could seriously impair their chances of eventual harmony and happiness.

He saw himself as a normal man, without sight. But Marion, looking at his blinded eyes, saw an abnormality that frightened and bewildered her. She thought she could have coped with his blindness had his sightless eyes been covered with their lids, like two little shutters over darkened windows. But his eyes had not lost their dark, penetrating gleam. It was uncanny the way he seemed to be always watching her, and disconcerting, too, for she knew she was always deceiving him.

Sheba had been the 'last straw'. Why should she pretend to like this huge dog when she was scared to death? Couldn't he understand it was the 'last straw' – or hadn't he any imagination?

'Thank you, Matron. I'll be getting along now,' he told her, when he had finished smoking the cigarette and drunk two cups of tea.

She wished him 'good luck', and hoped he would enjoy his evening swim. It was high tide at six o'clock. Then he went to his bedroom to collect a towel, and to change into trunks, shorts and jersey, before going down to the beach. Sheba was puzzled by his lack of excitement that evening, and she waited in vain for the joyous shout – 'Come on in! – It's marvellous!'

The beach was deserted, and she followed him into the water, with a premonition of danger, for he was behaving so strangely, and had not spoken a word since they left Matron's office.

They swam out further than usual, that evening, and Sheba was panting and struggling to keep abreast with the flaying arms. Richard was a strong swimmer.

But he did not struggle when cramp clawed at his legs in the cold currents. It would be sweet to die in the arms of his mistress.

Some time later, he was stretched on the beach, and Sheba was standing over him, pawing his heaving chest.

'Get off my blasted chest! I can't breathe,' he growled.

Within the reach of his outflung hands he could feel the tide lapping the shore, and he rolled over, buried his face in the sand, and sobbed.

3

Andy McLaren, at forty, was still a bachelor, and still determined to remain one, for he thoroughly enjoyed his life the way he lived it, and he hadn't to please anyone but himself – and, of course, the 'old man'!

The 'old man' – Master of the S.S. *Hebrides* – was almost due for retirement, and Andy was expecting promotion in the near future.

As First Mate of the *Hebrides*, with twenty years' service with the company, he was next in line for a ship's command, but he was not particularly ambitious, and was happy enough in his present position, so long as they didn't move him again. That was the only complaint he had against the company. As soon as you got attached to your ship and acquainted with the ship's company, you were informed of a change.

Looking back over that long period of years, he remembered most vividly his first sea voyage on the old *Braemar*. She was sunk back in 1944. Sometimes he would stand on the bridge during the night watch, in mid-ocean, and see the cruel havoc of that unforgettable night re-enacted, so vividly, he was bathed in sweat. Nothing had so impressed itself on his mind in all the rest of his adventurous seafaring life.

He could still see those gaping holes in the boat deck, hear the groans of trapped men, and the terrified screams of women and children. In a pool of blood, 'young Sparks' was lying dead, still wearing his ear-phones.

Richard Seal, staggering like a drunken man, with a

hand flung across his eyes, was yelling 'Where is everyone? What's happened? I can't see a blasted thing!'

After twenty years, Andy was still haunted by the memory, and the awful conviction that the blast which had blinded Richard was meant for himself. He could swear it was meant for him. How else could you explain the fact that he should have been standing in exactly that position, if he hadn't been five minutes late on duty that night?

As Fourth Mate, he was due to take over the watch at eight bells, but he had been disgustingly seasick all day, and could hardly stand on his feet on the rolling deck. This was his first sea voyage, and he was finding it more difficult than most to find his 'sea-legs'.

Young Jamie Ferguson, the Sixth Engineer, was also suffering in the same humiliating way, and they hardly dared to show their faces, for the ragging only seemed to add insult to injury. They had both tried to cover up their indisposition, but the quarters were too cramped for privacy, and there was no escape from anyone, they soon learned to their cost, once they had embarked on an ocean voyage. Whatever happened you had to grin and bear it!

Andy was a stocky, freckle-faced youth, with an earnest desire to see the world at the expense of the shipping company at Liverpool. He hadn't reckoned on mine-infested waters, or dark convoys in mid-Atlantic, though, when he signed on for service. Neither had he reckoned with a sickness so violent it left him weak and exhausted. But for the friendly encouragement of Richard Seal, the Third Mate, Andy supposed he would have given up the ghost, or slipped quietly overboard during the worst of the storms.

Richard was one of those admirable characters who take to the sea like a duck to water. He was 'tall, dark and handsome' – according to the young stewardess, Elizabeth Davies, commonly known as 'Liz'. Poor Liz. She was on her first voyage too, and 'sick as a dog' they told him. She was also under a bit of a cloud, it seemed, for the senior stewardesses were hardened sailors and had no time or sympathy to spare for a young subordinate.

Richard Seal was a man's man, with scant interest in the opposite sex, so Andy had gathered from the ship's company, until it leaked out some six months ago that he had secretly married an aspiring young actress, at Chelsea Registry Office. It had been quite a 'nine days wonder' apparently, for Richard had a reputation as an athlete and sportsman, but not as a lady-killer.

To Andy, however, on this first voyage, Richard was superb. His dark, magnetic eyes could be hard as steel, or tender as a woman's. His lean face was tanned by sun and wind, and he revelled in wild weather and rough seas. The tropics, he declared, were not for him, and he thought of signing on for an arctic expedition after the war! He had not seemed at all surprised to find himself in mid-Atlantic, and had even suggested it might be 'quite exciting'.

Quite exciting? Oh, my God! Andy would remember that stricken face for the rest of his life, and that dark, arrogant head silhouetted against the red glow of the sky.

They had kept in touch through the years, and Andy divided his shore leaves between Inverness, with his parents, and visiting Richard. He had stayed at the same hotel at Rottingdean, since the end of the war, to be near Richard, when he went back to Ovingdean for holidays. It was a friendship they both valued, for they still spoke the same language – the language of seafaring men.

Richard had promised himself a long sea voyage 'when my ship comes home', but somehow or other money had been scarce, and he had been tied up for years with a business which provided a livelihood, but lacked that spark of excitement and adventure so essential to a man of Richard's calibre.

Andy had been a reluctant witness on several occasions to the tragedy of that hurried wartime marriage, and spent weekends in a crowded flat in which Richard seemed ridiculously like a dog in a kennel. To Andy, who had seen the man in his rightful setting, it was pitiful and sad. Yet, nobody was really to blame – Richard had laughed at Andy's confession to being five minutes late on watch that fateful night, and its bitter significance – and told him not to talk such damn rot! St Dunstan's had done their best. Richard Seal was a splendid example of the new age of blindness – a bold and independent personality, not a groping, frightened man. But even Andy could see he was not an easy person to live with any more, and Andy was the first to make excuses for the discord and disharmony that seemed to arise out of the smallest trifles. The atmosphere, in that crowded flat, even to Andy's phlegmatic nature, was so charged with emotion, nothing seemed quite natural any more. Richard was either profoundly cheerful or morose as a bear. And Marion, quite obviously, was scared of him in his blackest moods. Andy was sorry for both, but always relieved when the visit was over. The bond between these two was near breaking point many years ago, and only held together by Marion's frequent absences, and Richard's holidays at Ovingdean, Andy had realised.

In so many ways, even the blinded Richard was unsuited to marriage, for he hadn't the capacity to lose himself in the nature of another being – though he thought he had! He was too much of an egoist, too much a law unto himself. Blindness had not changed this fundamental characteristic, though it had changed the gentle qualities of sympathy, tenderness and understanding. They no longer existed for him, and a harshness had taken their place. No wonder his wife was torn between anger and admiration! In a way, it was understandable, for Richard's moods and behaviour could be most unpredictable, even downright objectionable sometimes. But it was impossible to find happiness together when both were so completely absorbed in self.

Yet Richard's love was a contradiction of all his strong independence, for he clung to the illusion of love long after it was dead.

This, to Andy, was pathetic and degrading, for a man of Richard's stature. Sheba had absorbed much of this demanding love of Richard's, for her clever canine instinct recognised the man's absolute superiority. It was better so, Andy reflected, when he saw the humble devotion in the dog's eyes the first time they met. Surely in this new relationship, such trusting devotion must bring its compensations?

Andy was in Singapore when he read the brief account of the divorce and Marion's re-marriage to her leading man, Clive Baker. Although he had been expecting it for years, he was still shocked, and never more anxious to get back to England, to see for himself how Richard had reacted to this further devastating blow.

He knew they had a very capable housekeeper – Marion had seen to that – and he was not without friends. Ovingdean, as always, would be a temporary refuge, but this break-up of his marriage would need a different sort of courage. Was there a limit to a man's endurance, even a man like Richard Seal?

A cablegram to Ovingdean assured Andy, however, that Richard was staying there with Sheba, and was fit and cheerful. Well, he hadn't really expected anything else – Richard had guts! What would he do now? It would be the end of a way of life that had grown familiar to a blinded man. Where would he find another absorbing occupation? If he was hoping for peace of mind, who, but himself, could provide it? Somehow it seemed hardly appropriate yet, to this vigorous and vital friend of his. Peace of mind would come later, perhaps, when he had conquered new worlds.

He was still a young man, and life was not finished because a woman had been unfaithful.

They were floating lazily, some fifty yards from the shore, one Summer evening – with Sheba sitting guard over their shorts, jerseys and shoes – when Richard told Andy of his new plans. Andy turned his head slowly and his kind grey eyes searched the familiar lines of the lean, handsome face. Both admiration and amusement were there, in his searching glance.

'Good show!' was his only comment, for he was a man sparing of words, but Richard understood, for he stuck out his chin and grinned, looking very pleased with himself.

'You know, I've often thought I should like to write a book, but I've been much too occupied earning a living,' he confessed, 'Now that I've managed to save a bit, well, enough to keep me going for twelve months or so, I'm going to have a bash! A year of living like a hermit, with Sheba, and somebody to do a bit of cooking and cleaning, is just what I need. I've been getting much too complacent lately, and I need something bracing for a change. Any new challenge is bracing, don't you agree, old chap?'

'Profoundly,' said Andy, his eyes twinkling. 'But why go all the way to the Cotswolds to rent a remote cottage? Surely the agent could have done better than that?'

'I told him I wanted to get as far away as possible from my present surroundings, and he took me at my word, that's all. What's wrong with the Cotswolds? I shall take a look at Devon and Cornwall while I'm down there. I've always had a hankering after the West Country, as you know; I might even settle down there eventually. In the meantime, I enjoy long train journeys, so does Sheba – is she all right? Cast an eye on her, there's a good chap.'

'She's all right, but I suspect she is getting a wee bit

worried. Perhaps we ought to be getting back? She doesn't altogether trust me to keep an eye on you!'

(She's remembering what happened the last time we came here, Richard thought, but nobody but Sheba would ever know about that narrow escape from death.)

'I can still get back to Ovingdean for the Summer holiday, and Christmas. Perhaps you could manage to get down to me one weekend – when you get back from Singapore?'

'Aye, I will,' Andy agreed, mildly, as though he were just taking a little trip to Brighton!

It was always the same when they got together, for distance was covered in the memory, not in miles, in the company of those with whom you had travelled. Richard still spoke of 'seeing' things, for his mind's eye reflected the people and places of his youth. Revisiting Devon and Cornwall, he would 'see' it through the vivid eyes of memory.

'It's going to be fascinating getting it all down on paper, and watching it grow. One has to be pretty methodical, I should imagine, in writing a book. Anyway, I shall have to concentrate, and that will take my mind off other things,' Richard reflected.

A shadow passed over his mobile face, and, for a long moment, he was struggling again with the demon of self-pity. Then suddenly he rolled over and shouted: 'Come on – you lazy Son-of-a-Gun! Race you to the shore!'

Andy took up the challenge, but could not catch up with those strong flaying arms. He was out of practice, and never a very enthusiastic swimmer, even in the heated pool on board ship! He could see Sheba still standing guard over their clothes, but now her tail was swishing, excitedly. A few yards offshore, Richard lifted his head and called, 'Sheba! Come!'

She instantly obeyed that compelling voice, and swam out boldly to meet him, for now she knew her fears were groundless, and he was coming back. The anguish of that long, lonely vigil on the beach had been almost unbearable. But he had commanded her to stay, and she knew no other way of life than to obey his commands. The excitement and pleasure in her great, plunging body was so touching. Andy's throat tightened with an emotion too strong for words. If human relationships had failed Richard, he could still know the loyalty and devotion of this strangely gentle creature. They were greeting each other now, like two long-lost friends, and their wet, shining faces were singularly alike at the moment of reunion.

Back at the cottage, Richard set himself a target of one thousand words a day. 'The Sea Was My Mistress' was absorbing all his time now, and he thought of nothing else.

'I've a one-track mind,' he told Beth. 'It must be all or nothing.'

He didn't ask her opinion of the pages of typescript she read aloud before she left for home. If he was not completely satisfied, he tore it up and dropped it in the waste paper basket. He needed no other critic but himself. It was a man's world he was writing about, and women played no part in it.

On the way to the village, one afternoon, to buy a fresh supply of paper for the typewriter, Richard suddenly halted to ask Sheba, anxiously, 'What's the matter, girl? Why are you limping?'

Dropping to his knees, he took up her paws, one by one, and carefully examined them. On the left foreleg, he discovered a large swelling, and when he pressed it gently, he could feel the shiver of pain vibrating in his own fingers.

'That's a nasty abscess,' he told her sympathetically. 'Poor old girl, what rotten luck. Can you manage to get as far as the village, do you think? Then I can phone the vet from the post office.'

Sheba pushed her head between his knees, whimpering like a child.

'We can take it in easy stages.' His voice was kind and reassuring.

Then he stood up, took hold of the white harness, and they went forward together, matching their steps slowly and carefully. Their steps were measured to Sheba's halting limp, and it was dusk when they reached the village. She was limping badly now, and children hurrying home from school stopped to ask anxiously, 'What's the matter with Sheba? Has she got a bad foot?'

'She's got an abscess on her paw, and it's very painful,' he told them.

Children were seldom embarrassed by his blindness, Richard had noticed, and they chatted away quite naturally, They would sometimes ask if they could see him across the road, and he would thank them politely, but explain it was Sheba's job to do that. Obviously they were very impressed by her cleverness, and found it difficult to believe she could actually take her master to the right shop, and all the way back, without any help other than a single word of command: 'Forward'.

'Sheba's on duty when she's wearing her white harness, so you mustn't touch her,' Richard had told them when they crowded round the first time he took her to the village. Their voices followed him into the post office –

'Poor Sheba, she's got an abscess on her paw.'

They all seemed very concerned about her.

The post-mistress looked up the vet's number, and Richard was conscious of the sudden awkward silence in the office as he went into the call box to dial the number. It was easy, there was nothing to it, and he felt a little irritated by their mild curiosity. And why did so many sighted people invariably suppose he was deaf, when his hearing was so acutely sensitive, he could actually feel the vibration of a bird's wings, and the soughing of wind in the branches. In loud, penetrating voices, people would discuss his blindness and his 'handicap' with a queer sort of relish, and he would deliberately 'show off' his cleverness, in one way or another, to get his revenge!

The vet promised to come along and collect them within a few minutes, which he did. The abscess, he said, would have to be lanced, and then he would run them home in his car. In the vet's surgery, Sheba was given an injection, and the paw bathed in antiseptic. Under his sensitive fingers, Richard could feel the quivering flesh, and then, a moment later, the stench in his nostrils. The abscess was his own, and the stench was his own, so closely were they linked together. He felt a little sick and giddy when it was over, and was glad of the drink the vet offered him before they started for home.

'It's the first time anything like this has happened, and it's a bit upsetting,' he confessed. 'It's my own fault for not checking on her paws when I groomed her last night. What caused it, and how can I prevent it happening again?'

'I should say it was probably a scratch, or a small wound that got infected with a thorn – but it's nothing to worry about, and Sheba's in such splendid shape it will heal quickly. I am putting on a little pad with strapping to keep it in place. Don't remove it, I'll look in later in the week. Well, I'm ready if you are?'

'Thanks. I'm ready.'

'There's a light in your cottage,' the vet told Richard, as they turned into the lane.

'That's odd. Oh well, I'm not worried. If it's a burglar, Sheba will soon scare the daylights out of him!' laughed Richard, as they climbed out of the car.

'Sure you wouldn't like me to investigate?'

'No thanks. We shall be all right, it was good of you to bring us back.'

The other man's hand was broad and strong and his grip was hard.

'It's a pleasure. I've often admired that dog of yours – and you too, for that matter. Well, look after yourselves! Good-night.'

A woman's voice called anxiously into the darkness.

'Is that you, Mr Seal?'

'Yes, it's me,' Richard's voice called back. 'What are you doing here, Beth? It's after six o'clock.'

'Yes, I know, but I couldn't leave till I saw you safely back. What happened?'

Richard's reply was lost as the door closed, but the vet's curiosity was aroused. Beth? That must be Beth Walker, he decided, as he backed the car down the lane. Well, I don't envy her with those two! – a couple of thoroughbreds, but temperamental as prima donnas, I shouldn't wonder!

"You shouldn't have bothered, it wasn't necessary,' Richard told her shortly, as he sank into a chair and stretched his legs to the blazing fire.

'I was worried.' Her voice was strained, and she seemed upset.

But he was not concerned with her, or her lone cycle ride to the village through the dark lanes. He wanted to be rid of her now. Pulling Sheba between his knees, he clasped his hands under her warm belly, and asked gently, 'Feeling better, girl?'

His face in the firelight was strangely beautiful.

"Good night,' said Beth softly. She was crying as she pedalled down the lane.

The following morning, when Beth pushed her bicycle to the shed behind the cottage, she found Tom Little on the roof, and Richard standing at the foot of the ladder, his face raised inquiringly. Sheba, in a state of great agitation, blocked the doorway, and both were surrounded by little heaps of dirty, dusty thatch, which Tom was quietly dislodging from the leaking patch.

'Watch yerself now, Sir, there's more coming down,' he warned, his weather-beaten face puckered anxiously. 'Must get rid of the old stuff first,' he explained.

Richard, as always, was impatient of delay, and this further interruption to his strict routine, and the new target he had set himself, was making him restless and irritable. He wouldn't stay indoors, but Beth could see he was going to hinder rather than help the man on the roof.

'Good morning, Tom!' she called out brightly, and Richard swung round.

'Oh, is that you, Beth – we are in one hell of a mess here today. This rotten old thatch is full of dust,' he choked.

'So would you be, Sir, if you'd been sitting on this 'ere roof for nigh on fifty year!' chuckled Tom.

'Fifty years!' Richard exploded. 'No wonder it's leaking, man! It's a positive disgrace! The landlord should be compelled to keep his property weather-proof, if nothing else. And why wasn't I warned this could happen?'

Tom and Beth exchanged a smile, for they both knew the eccentric old landlord who owned a number of old cottages, and had not been near his property since the war. He employed an agent to collect his rents once a month.

'I done a patching job on this 'ere roof once afore, but I ain't never done the job proper, stripping off to the rafters, and I be the only thatcher, Sir, round these parts. I been on thatching meself for nigh on fifty year, started with me ole Dad when I were twelve,' he added, proudly.

Richard prodded a lump of decayed thatch with the toe of his shoe, and muttered, indignantly, 'I should have been warned, it's a blinkin' disgrace! I hope you charge him up well for the job, Tom. Do him good to have a nice fat bill to pay!'

Tom's smile was slow and placid.

'Reckon I don't worry much about that. Nobody never made a fortune out of thatching. This 'ere patching don't give a chap no real pleasure, like when you can start from scratch, and see all the bare rafters. That's what I calls pleasure, Sir. With a whacking great 'eap of new straw, and them bare rafters waiting for it, I reckon I feel sort of – sort of – excited,' said Tom, searching for words.

'Like an artist looking at an empty canvas before he starts on a new picture,' Richard suggested blandly, from below.

Tom looked puzzled. His imagination didn't stretch that far, and he had never seen that sort of artist at work. He was tickled to death at some of the silly remarks he heard passed on his thatched roofs and hay ricks.

'The chap who did that is a real artist,' they would say, and 'Just look at that lovely roof, darling. Isn't it charming!'

His craft was a thing of beauty, and Tom was a craftsman to his fingertips. He was proud of his skill, not humble. It was a good, satisfying way of life, and he wouldn't have changed places with anyone. Bitterly disappointed in the three sons who obstinately refused an apprenticeship to thatching – and Tom was too mild a man to assert his authority – he still had hopes in his eldest grandson, who spent most of his holidays up and down the ladder, and had a 'feeling' for it – as Tom would say. You couldn't do without 'feeling', any more than a potter could mould a vase from a lump of clay. There was more to it than just covering a roof with straw, and decorating the eaves. You had to feel pride in your work. You had to enjoy your work so much you never wanted to take a holiday. That was the secret.

Beth had to step over Sheba for she wouldn't budge an inch. She was glad to have Richard out of the way, for it gave her an opportunity to clean the sitting-room thoroughly. Usually he was fidgeting around the place, and wanting to get back to work.

They had settled into a regular routine now, but it could be disturbed at any time by a sudden violent mood of ill-temper, or a day when nothing seemed to go according to plan, when Beth had to listen to the savage ripping of paper and Richard's curses. With an employer of Richard Seal's temperament, the job would never be without incident, never dull. But she knew she was giving more and more of herself, and they were demanding more. She was getting involved again, when she had promised herself to be immune from further involvement in other people's private lives. Richard and Sheba would drain her dry, and give nothing in return, for it wouldn't occur to them. Neither the man nor the dog had shown even the mildest curiosity in herself, as a person. Their close relationship excluded her even from the most casual friendship. They were neither friendly nor hostile, but completely disinterested. In six weeks, she was no closer to them than on her first day, and was constantly reminded by their arrogance and independence, they were merely tolerating her presence because she was useful. An insurmountable barrier divided them – a barrier she would try to break down in the months ahead, with her gentle persistence.

Every day now found her torn between hope and despair. Richard Seal had only to say one word of appreciation and she was blushing and trembling like a silly schoolgirl. Five minutes later she could be in tears. But if he was aware of her in either joy or distress, he did not reveal it. His hardness was as much an armour as her own reserve, she realised. The man behind the armour she saw in brief glimpses, and was so disturbed with love and longing, she had to walk away.

In the firelight, last evening, with his arms round Sheba, she had seen such tenderness and compassion in his face, it had been quite unbearable. Light and shade played over his mobile face so rapidly, she was constantly in doubt, and confused by his changing moods. But even that was preferable to the blankness of his shuttered face when he tried to control himself.

'I beg your pardon,' he would say, with forced contrition,

when she would feel loath to blame and eager to excuse anything he might say or do.

There was nothing to stop her from giving notice. She could pretend the two mile cycle ride was too arduous in the Winter months – but she couldn't leave him now.

Every morning found her shutting the door on Cindy, and her own quiet retreat, to hurry to that other place, where quietness was never peaceful, but a forced, unnatural compulsion to conquer a man's tempestuous moods. She had to pretend he needed her, and it was her duty to stay. But he didn't need her any more than he needed the butcher, or the baker, the coalman or the milkman. In her own way she was useful and necessary, but not indispensable – as she had hoped and expected to be when first they met. Any other woman would have suited him just as well, providing she would put up with his moods, and put everything back in its proper place. You hadn't to be clever or even a particularly good housekeeper – just amiable and obliging! It was humiliating to be nothing more than a useful pair of hands – humiliating and pathetic.

'I'm coming up with you, Tom. I want to see exactly what you are doing up there,' Richard announced, when they had finished dinner.

Tom pushed back his chair, wiped his hand across his mouth, and shrugged. He was wasting his breath to argue with a chap like Mr Seal. Beth thought so too.

'Just as you say, Sir,' he answered, winking at Beth. 'I'll put t'other ladder up alongside mine. It's a bit arkard on one ladder, and you're a big man.'

Richard was smiling confidently as he stood waiting, and Sheba was ordered to 'sit' on the doorstep.

'All ready, Sir,' called Tom, cheerily. 'Take it easy.'

They went up together, side by side – Richard gripping the rungs of the ladder, and Tom ready with a helping hand.

Bundles of clean, yellow straw lay ready on the roof, and one of these was put into Richard's hands.

'It's like this 'ere,' Beth heard Tom say, and then their voices were drowned by Sheba's frantic barking.

'Quiet!' yelled Richard from above. Sheba subsided into little moans of anguish, and buried her head in her paws.

Among the peculiar conglomeration of smells on the roof, Richard quickly detected the old sackcloth Tom had wrapped about his spindly legs, and a certain brand of tobacco he was chewing.

'I like a bit o' baccy, but it's too dangerous to smoke, with all this 'ere straw lying around – so I chews it instead,' Tom explained logically.

'Very sensible,' Richard agreed, pegging down a bundle of straw. 'Well, thanks for the lesson in thatching, Tom, but I don't think I'll take it on as a full-time occupation! I must get below now, and take that dog of mine for a walk. She sounds pretty miserable – can't stand anything a little unusual!' he laughed. 'Well, here we go. Half an hour's walk, then another three hour's work before tea.'

'What sort of work, Sir? – if I may make so bold?' Tom enquired.

'Writing a book,' said Richard, airily, stepping down the ladder.

"'Well I'll be durned!' said Tom, scratching his head.

4

Cindy's five puppies were all different, and she was inordinately proud of them. They were cross-bred pups, and had none of their mother's definite distinction and breeding.

'Aren't they adorable, Auntie Beth?' breathed the neighbour's twelve-year-old daughter, Jane. 'You will let me have one, won't you, when it's old enough to leave its mother?'

'Of course, dear, since you will be looking after them for me. Which one have you chosen, or haven't you decided?'

'The smallest, she's so sweet. I shall call her Susie, she looks like a Susie, doesn't she?'

'Yes, she does,' Beth agreed, as she mixed another bowl of bread and milk for Cindy, and left instructions for her midday dinner. With five babies to feed, she would need more than her usual morning and evening meal, she decided.

It was another dark, dreary December morning, with only ten days to Christmas. Jane was on her way to school, and Beth busy with her chores before setting out for Rose Cottage. The boiler was behaving better today, and the new delivery of Welsh nuts seemed to suit it, thank goodness. The kitchen was warm and comfortable for Cindy and her pups. The rest of the cottage was icy cold, for it was too dangerous to leave the oil heater burning all day, and the coal fire was laid ready in the sitting-room. She would light it on her return, and when the room had warmed, carry Cindy and the pups to the hearth rug, to spend the evening in the warm glow of fire light, at her feet.

She would tell Cindy all that happened at Rose Cottage,

and how the huge Alsatian lay stretched for hours at her master's feet, with her eyes fixed intently on his busy hands, and his strong, absorbed face. She talked to Cindy as easily and naturally as she would have talked to a human companion and, by doing so, suffered none of the repression or loneliness another woman might have known. She had never lived entirely alone, never experienced the awful silence of an empty house, when the door is pushed open and nothing stirs within but the frightened beat of a lonely heart.

Cindy's welcome was warm, and as tender as her soft brown eyes. Pixie, the one before Cindy, and a cross-bred Aberdeen terrier, had welcomed her with a barrage of excited barking. When the puppies were small, Beth stayed at home, and drew on her small savings, just for the joy of watching them grow, and to have them around the place. This was the first time she had entrusted the puppies to Jane, but she was a sensible child and good with animals. Cindy adored her – she was not exclusively Beth's dog, but had affection to spare for anyone who was kind to her.

Every dog she had known had been different in character and temperament. Each tiny puppy developed its own canine characteristics, in one way or another. Watching their growth with absorbed interest, Beth unconsciously satisfied the dormant maternity in her childless marriage.

It was a hard life now, with two old cottages to clean, and two homes to run, but Beth was not troubled by hardship. Soft living would not have suited her, and she had no desire for it.

Her big hands were blue with cold, the fingers chapped, and the blunt, unpolished nails splitting. In a thick tweed skirt and hand-knitted jumper, her tall, well-developed figure looked strong and sturdy. Her cheeks were tanned like a gypsy's with wind and rain; her mouth sweet and generous. Her soft, brown eyes revealed all that was gentle and kind and compassionate in her nature. Anger never darkened them. Jealousy and envy were passions unknown to her. She was a peaceful, undemonstrative woman, with a great depth of emotion concealed beneath the quiet dignity which surrounded her. Cruelty and cunning had no place in her thoughts or behaviour. She had no very decided views on anything, and was easily persuaded one way or the other. Yet she never gave the impression of weakness, rather the reverse, for a kind of stubborn pride, and a deep reserve, hid all her inhibitions.

Beth had few close friends, but many acquaintances in the village and beyond. Cindy was her closest companion – Cindy, the happy receiver of all her affection – the participator in all her simple pleasures, and the patient recipient of all her troubles.

She would spend three days at Christmas with a married brother in Somerset and his three children – Cindy and her pups would stay with Jane. Richard Seal would be away for a week with Sheba. They were going to Ovingdean.

She thought of him constantly now, and the two miles which separated them seemed to stretch farther and farther into obscurity. They may as well have been at the opposite ends of the earth for all the satisfaction it brought. She could never reach them – never touch them, for they were ever beyond the scope of her eager, outstretched hands. Enclosed in their private, protective shell, they were safe from her intrusion. Sometimes she found herself wishing she had taken the alternative job she had been offered in Wiltshire, for then she would have escaped the obligation to serve this man, and to be so disturbed by him. Her quiet contentment was already shattered by his masterful domination, and she was desperately afraid she would lose even the small measure of independence she still enjoyed, after Christmas. He had already hinted that he would like her to go in on Sunday morning to cook his dinner and wash up, as he was working seven days a week on his book. It was difficult to refuse – she had always found it easier to agree than refuse, even a sighted person's request. His blindness allowed him the advantage of being always on the receiving end, and of being completely selfish. He had not intended it to happen, was barely aware that it had happened, but over the years he had become so self-important he was no longer likeable. His manner rebuffed, rather than encouraged friendship, and Beth was no exception. If he was immune from her gentleness and devotion, she was not immune from his harshness and arrogance. He would probably despise her for being so agreeable – perhaps a disagreeable housekeeper would suit him better? She wondered whether he ever gave her a second's thought, once she had closed the door on Rose Cottage. Did he never wonder what she looked like? Whether she was tall or short, fat or thin, fair or dark? She supposed not, if he wasn't at all interested in her as a person – as a woman.

They had no contact at all without the sense of touch, and their hands never met over the table when she served his meal. They could continue this way for another six months, when he would be gone from Rose Cottage, and she would never see him again.

He was working to a close schedule he had told her, and the book must be finished before June, when the short lease on the cottage expired. He knew what he wanted to achieve in a limited time, and nothing but an earthquake would shake his resolution or change his plans.

Such determination was admirable, but unnerving to the one who watches such fierce concentration. Beth wondered if his nerves would crack under the strain. Perhaps she would crack first? She had all the distractions of a sighted person, while he, in his blindness, could assimilate his facts and assemble them quickly, with a mind uncluttered by other obligations. She would have liked to ask him whether memory was as fresh without sight, and whether he remembered colour, and pattern, shape and size, with accuracy or with insight. Was red still red and green still green? Was his world completely dark, or had it light and shade – like his shadowed face? She was shut out, would always be shut out from his world of blindness, yet she longed to share it. If she could only be his eyes! But Sheba was his eyes.

If she could walk beside him, and he would grip her hand as lightly as he gripped the handle of the white harness he could re-discover so much of beauty he had lost, for Sheba's eyes were earth bound, and clouds and sky, sunset and sunrise, trees and flowers, and waving corn, had no meaning for her. The warmth of the sun and the direction of the wind would have new meaning.

What did he see now, beyond the orbit of those dark, magnetic eyes?

She would like to know.

She would like to understand.

Every day she was wondering about the countless things he must be missing so intolerably in his sightless world, and surely the sea must be the greatest loss to a seafaring man? With this on her mind she questioned him one morning over the dinner table.

'Have you never thought of swimming in the river, or is it too dangerous?'

'It's too static, nothing can compare with the sea,' he sighed. I get a bit of practice at Ovingdean, of course, and I've won the championship outright three times, but then I had an advantage over the other chaps, being a naval officer. The swimming pool on board ship is not very spacious, but it's enough to keep you in trim. I've often had it to myself after the four hour night watch, and felt like a blinkin' Rothschild.'

'Yes, I know – I mean, I can imagine it.'

The clatter of a dish surprised him. It was the first time Beth had broken anything, and she was so profuse in her apologies she was almost in tears.

'How could I be so careless – and one of your best dinner plates, too,' she was saying contritely.

'Forget it,' he laughed carelessly, but the incident disturbed him. Why did he make her so nervous?

The hole in his sock had been mended, and the missing button on his shirt had been replaced by another. Richard noticed these things, but said nothing.

Wherever he went, women wanted to fuss over him, to do things for him – out of pity for his blindness. His resentment would grow to a white heat of suffocation in his chest, and he would walk Sheba for miles, away from people; away from the obligation to accept their charity – for pity was charity. Any solitary place, with Sheba, restored the balance of his mind and spirit.

In the years when his living had depended on the little tobacconist's shop, and he clung to familiar surroundings with a desperate hope of reconciliation with Marion, he managed, on the whole, to keep his resentment under control during business hours. But when he had pulled down the blind and locked the shop door, he often boarded a bus, and travelled to its farthest destination in order to relieve himself of this terrible burden of resentment.

Pity! Why should they pity him?

Why was it so impossibly difficult to convince anyone that he was a *normal man without sight* – not a helpless imbecile, or a deaf mute!

God! – it was awful!

Even in Andy he sometimes detected a kind of pity – blast him!

Yet only Andy understood his craving for space, and freedom of movement – only Andy realised he was still fundamentally the same man. The changes Andy saw in him were only superficial. Blindness was superficial. Insight and instinct had replaced his normal vision. That was all. His senses were so highly developed, and his intellect so sharpened by blindness, he was actually a better man, a more intelligent man in maturity, than in his sighted youth.

Space and freedom of movement – he had Sheba to thank for this. Marion had been too busy, and Andy, when he came ashore, too lazy!

Pulling on his socks, and buttoning up his shirt that morning, Richard was conscious, for the first time, of his housekeeper's quiet persistence. She had apparently ignored his 'Leave it! That's my job!' – and not for the first time. Beth was cunning! He must watch his step or she would be intruding too far on his jealously guarded independence. He smiled sardonically, as he straightened his tie.

Sheba was stretching and yawning at the open door, and he slapped her backside with a hard hand. She spun round, and playfully nipped the back of his hand. She seemed to be laughing at him.

'Go on, mock me! It's all very well for you, for you haven't to cope with these blasted females!" he told her savagely.

Then he took hold of her, and pushed her roughly to the floor, and they wrestled together, rolling over and over in a fierce embrace. Sheba's panting breath was hot on his face. She was quivering with excitement, like a young puppy. Without the white harness, she often experienced this sense of fun and freedom, and a great desire to roll on her back and growl. It was a long, long time since her master had been so playful, though, and she was so taken by surprise, she was momentarily stunned by his behaviour.

He was always unpredictable, but she had taught herself to accept anything and everything from this man, who seemed, to her canine intelligence, the supreme authority.

Her paw had healed nicely, and the abscess completely disappeared, but Sheba remembered her master's tenderness and compassion during that agonising walk to the village, when she had met the vet for the first time. Why, he had even tried to carry her, at one stage of the journey! She worshipped the ground he walked on, and he could do no wrong in her trusting heart. Whatever happened, she must never leave him. This was the object of all her extensive training, and her very existence. She was aware of it, and the heavy responsibility it entailed, every hour of the day and night. But only when she was released from the white harness could she enjoy the wild ecstasy in her blood and her very loins. For a few glorious moments, on the wide heath, or an open field, released from her bondage, she would feel the strongest urge to run and run. Her master's shrill, prolonged whistle would catch her in joyous flight and she would stop dead, then turn around and bound back to him.

'I know exactly how you feel, my beauty,' he told her, compassionately, one day, as he slipped on the white harness. 'I often feel the same wild desire to run and run, but where should I find myself?'

She remembered how gentle his voice had been that day, and that all his pride and arrogance had been momentarily deflated. But Sheba, back in the white harness, was no longer divided by conflicting emotions. Her duty was plain, and her loyalty unquestioned. She wished him to understand she was quite content to serve him for the rest of her days.

It was Sunday morning – the Sunday before Christmas – when they rolled on the floor, in sudden, young excitement. Richard was laughing and panting.

'Hey! Stop it, will you, Sheba! I'm getting too old for this sort of thing!' he gasped, pushing her roughly away.

Scrambling to his feet, he stood at the open window, breathing in great gulps of cold air. How he loved the Winter! It was going to be a white Christmas according to the weather forecast on the wireless. They might even get some sledging on the hills if they were lucky! Running his fingers through his stiff hair, he stretched luxuriously, and felt strangely exhilarated by the prospect of a white Christmas. So many of recent years had been mild and damp.

The weather, as always, played an important part in his way of life. The elements, to a seafaring man – and he still considered himself a seafaring man – were so closely embodied in his senses and environment, he was always aware of them, even a little in awe of them, when they raged in a storm.

It was blowing hard from the north-east today, stinging his cheeks. The bare branches of the elm tree flapped noisily, like human arms beating together for warmth. Sparrows chirped in the eaves. Tom Little had done a good job on the roof, and there was no further trouble. A dog howled dismally some distance away. He thought it was chained to an outside kennel, for he sometimes heard it howling in the night, when he lay awake. But sleepless nights were getting to be almost a rarity, and he seldom thought of Marion these days. She was out of his life and out of his system, for good! God! – but it was grand to feel free again!

He stuck his head out of the window, and the wind tore at his hair and billowed his shirt and trousers. He flung out his arms, and the first flakes of snow fell softly on his upturned face. Sheba stood beside him with her paws on the window sill, and together they listened to the bells of the village church, ringing for the ten o'clock family service.

'I wonder if Beth is on her way to church?' The thought was involuntary and quite unexpected. Richard pushed it away, impatiently, and pulled a thick woollen sweater over his head.

'Come on, girl. Work!' he told her authoritatively.

And Sheba followed him obediently down the stairs.

They were an hour later on Sunday morning, sitting down to the big old-fashioned desk Richard had brought from the flat. It was the only piece of furniture he possessed, for Marion had rented and furnished the new flat when he was still at St Dunstan's. Before the divorce was made absolute, he had received a letter from her solicitor, offering him the entire contents of their former home, but he was not interested. Property and possessions had little value to a man like Richard. Marion had forgotten that, or perhaps never realised it. They were miles apart. It was not her fault, but her misfortune, that Fate had kept her tied for so long to a man who had no appreciation of material values. Soft carpets, pretty draperies, a cocktail cabinet, contemporary-styled furniture, gilt-edged mirrors, a few pictures by modern artists, and a large collection of dolls in costume from the various countries Marion had visited on tour with the company – these were all her possessions, but they had no meaning for Richard.

He was just not interested.

At one time he had been attracted to small porcelain figures, and had a collection, of no great value, he had picked up in antique shops and street markets, as far apart as Bristol and Bombay. These had been broken surreptitiously by a long succession of dailies at the flat, in the early years of their life together.

Eventually, however, there was nothing left to remind Marion she had married a seafaring man but this big, old-fashioned desk she privately considered a monstrosity! It had been fashioned, most lovingly, by 'Chips', the ship's carpenter, during the long hours in foreign ports, and presented to the young officer he had so respected and admired. The tang of the sea still clung to its timbers – or was it imagination? Tidily and methodically Richard had filed invoices and letters, in the days when he was responsible for buying and stock-taking the tobacconist's shop.

But nothing today remained of that particular chapter of his life.

The present chapter, devoted exclusively to the compiling

of a single volume of memoirs – 'The Sea Was My Mistress' – was uncluttered by reminders of that soul-destroying decade. His equipment was cut to the absolute minimum now – a desk, a typewriter, a good supply of paper and his own concentrated efforts – that was all!

However, Sunday mornings, without a housekeeper, held certain obligations and disadvantages before he could settle down to work. With a dressing-gown over his pyjamas, and his hair still tousled from sleep, he went downstairs with Sheba, on the stroke of eight. This precise punctuality had been another bone of contention between them in the old days, for Marion had no sense of time, and was invariably late for her appointments.

For Richard, the days and nights were still measured in 'watches' and 'bells'. He still could not break the habits of his youth, and the braille watch on his wrist held the same reminder to punctuality as the ship's clock on the bridge.

So, on the stroke of eight, he was putting on his slippers and tying the belt of the expensive dressing-gown, which had been his wife's last present on his forty-second birthday.

The first chore he faced reluctantly, for it smothered him in dust, and he was so fastidiously particular about his appearance that he could not bear to think he might leave black smudges on his clothes from his soiled hands. But the dead ashes had to be cleared from the grate, and a fresh supply of wood and coal brought in from the shed before they could enjoy a fire. Sheba would stand well back during these Sunday morning wrestling matches with the old-fashioned stove, for her master's irritation was evident in his glowering face, and his hands. He attacked the job with the air of a man who detests the very nature of stoves and dead ashes! – cursing and frowning when impatient fingers dislodged a bar, or spilt ashes in the hearth.

'Get out of my way!' he yelled at Sheba, as he flung the fender aside, with such violence she was obliged to crouch against the wall, where she stayed, watching his movements with anxious eyes. She could never understand just why he found this particular chore so troublesome, when he was clever at other, far more exacting tasks, such as cooking breakfast and supper, washing up, chopping and sawing wood, trimming hedges, and sweeping dead leaves from the garden paths. Sheba rather dreaded Sunday mornings in the old cottage when they had no housekeeper, and this unpleasant task faced them as they came downstairs. Richard would fling open the back door and vigorously shake the hearth rug. That would be the signal for battle! But, with the crackle of wood, and the spurt of flames up the chimney, his irritation vanished. Squatting on his heels, holding out his blackened hands to the blazing fire, he told Sheba, contradictorily, 'You see how easy it is? I don't know why people make such a fuss – there's nothing to it! Come here, girl!' – and she would join him on the hearth rug, and squat beside him, with her great lolling tongue licking at the firelight.

The flames would be reflected in the highly-polished surface of the stove, for Richard never failed to find the black-lead brush in the cupboard under the stairs. The cement hearth would dry quickly in the heat, under the brass fender. There would be smudges on her master's cheeks and forehead, and his tousled head would be full of dust. But he never touched her with his blackened hands, knowing that she, too, was extremely fastidious about her appearance.

'Now we must check on the boiler – then we can take a bath!' he would say, and the immediate prospect of a bath seemed to cheer him up enormously. But the kitchen boiler presented no problem, for the housekeeper cleared it out thoroughly on Saturday morning, and thereafter, for the rest of the week, it required nothing more than a hod of small coke, morning and evening, and the dust riddled out twice a day. The whole operation, on Sunday morning, took less than ten minutes, then Richard, whistling a shrill tune, washed his hands at the kitchen sink.

On the Sunday before Christmas, as he dried his hands on the roller towel, he said, thoughtfully, to Sheba, 'Shall we ask Beth to come in Sunday morning, or not? I can't make up my mind. In one way it would save all this bother and mess, but, on the other hand, we should lose a lot of our independence, and we don't want to be fussed too much. It's bad for us. What do you think? Shall we carry on as usual, and manage without her?'

Sheba barked twice, decisively, and Richard laughed.

'Just as you say, my beauty! We carry on as usual. On the whole I rather enjoy being on our own, for we haven't to put on an act to please anyone. It's a bit of a strain, old girl, six days a week, having to behave ourselves! We are not naturally docile or domesticated creatures, you and I, and we don't conform to pattern, that's the trouble. Beth would like to tame me, I expect. I don't know – she's a bit of a mystery. I can't make her out. She seems unnaturally quiet and agreeable. I should rather like to know her honest opinion of you and me, Sheba. I'll bet it would be illuminating! What do we care!' – and he laughed harshly.

Sheba followed him into the bathroom, where he quickly stepped out of his dressing-gown and pyjamas, and flung them over the back of the chair. Then he kicked off his slippers, knowing that Sheba would collect them up and hold them carefully between her paws. She was very proud of this achievement, but it was one of many Richard had taught her. Her next objective was the large bath towel, draped over the hot tank, and she kept an eye on it, ready to seize it in her jaws when her master was ready. He liked a lot of water in his bath, and Sheba shared his enjoyment, in spite of all the splashings and the cloud of steam that almost obscured her vision. She loved to see him so relaxed and happy, and he always sang in his bath, in a deep, unmelodious voice, snatches of Gilbert and Sullivan and 'Old Man River' – never very sure of the words, and making them up as he went along. He had no ear for music, but liked to hear a military band on the wireless, or Nat King Cole.

His long, lean body, submerged in the water, seemed to lose all its tenseness. He would take the soap and vigorously wash the dust from his hair – then plunge his head in the water, again and again, till it poured from his ears, and wet shining face, in a stream. This was his true element – water – not earth, and when he shouted for his towel, more than half an hour had passed – and the bathroom floor was flooded!

With breakfast over, and the washing-up done, Richard went straight into the sitting-room, with a fresh pot of coffee, and sat down at his desk. Sheba had been out in the garden for ten minutes while he washed the dishes, and she came to the back door immediately in answer to his whistle. She knew exactly what she had to do next, without any reminder. As she stretched on the floor, prepared for a long vigil, her master's hand reached down to stroke her head, and ran the length of her big, powerful body. It was more a caress than a pat, and she shivered in an ecstasy of joy and contentment, for now the hours would pass pleasantly in his company, and while he worked, she would dream her canine dreams, watching his busy fingers on the keyboard. She knew, by instinct that the work which claimed so many hours of their day was far more absorbing and exacting than the other work to which she had grown accustomed. In their present surroundings, this small machine with its clattering keys and tinkling bell, was the centre of his industry.

Sheba had been puzzled for some time by the new order of things, when they first moved to the cottage, and confused by the importance of this curious object to which her master seemed so attached. Behind the counter, in the shop, he had been constantly interrupted in his packing and unpacking by customers, but he seemed not to mind in the least. Sheba had been allowed to walk about, and even stand in the shop doorway, to be admired by passing pedestrians. But here, in the cottage, it was different. Their working schedule was confined to this one room, in which she had to acquaint herself with long hours of silence, interrupted only by the tinkling bell, and the strange, staccato hammering of the keys.

Nothing must be allowed to disturb this extraordinary concentration. A bark was strictly forbidden, even a yawn or a growl frowned upon. During the early weeks of this enforced stillness, Sheba had endured the pangs of cramp in all her limbs, and an awful sense of boredom, unrelieved by anything more exciting than the housekeeper's feet padding quietly from the kitchen to the stairs. Her master's face would register bitterness, amusement, scorn, as his hands flew swiftly over the keys. He was a law unto himself, and Sheba, who knew him best, would be the first to suffer the insults of his biting tongue, or the anger on his darkened face, when a black mood of despair took its hold on him.

The snow fell softly, and the world all about them was touched with magic. Richard would discover it later in the day, when he opened the door and walked out into the garden.

The period of which he was writing was far removed from this wintry setting, for memory had served to remind him that morning of the Red Sea, shimmering under a tropical sun, and his limp shirt, drenched with sweat, clinging to his hairy chest. He could see 'Old Sparks' with a scarlet face, and sleeves rolled over his elbows. His fat, sagging stomach stretched the seams of his tight, cotton trousers. A small electric fan gently stirred the few remaining hairs on his near-bald head. Dear 'Old Sparks' – what a character!

'Young Sparks', who revelled in the sun, and asked nothing more of life than to sail for ever on a tropical sea, was looking as cool as a cucumber in the stifling little wireless cabin on the boat deck. He was always immaculately dressed, never removed his tie, and his white uniform, even in the Red Sea, was as fresh and uncreased as when it was delivered from the Liverpool laundry. He was Richard's age, but seemed much younger. They had nothing in common, but a rather vulgar taste for fish and chips. 'Young Sparks' was blond and blue-eyed and pretty as a girl.

'The Second' of the six engineers aboard the old *Astoria* was in his late forties – a hefty giant of a man, with a vile temper and a fist that could fell an ox. He had no home ashore, and no background other than the sea and the ships in which he served. Under his protection, 'Young Sparks' was spared all manner of unpleasant incidents and ragging, a maiden voyage normally promised, for they were all scared to touch him for fear of reprisals. So the bland look of innocence was never once removed from his face on this, his first voyage, as a junior wireless operator – until they docked at Bombay, when he was discovered, in the early hours of Sunday morning, blind drunk and abandoned on the summit of Malabar Hill! Since nobody was held responsible, and the rest of the crew swore they had spent the evening either at the Club or the cinema, the 'Second's' blazing wrath was confined to awful threats should the culprit's name ever be divulged!

Obviously 'Young Sparks' had been taken to the terrace at the summit of Malabar Hill to admire the view of the city in one of those horse-drawn gharries, so familiar in the streets of Bombay. And Richard, who had a great reputation for practical jokes and midnight pranks in hired gharries, was generally assumed to be the culprit!

A flicker of amusement passed over the face of the middle-aged Richard, recalling this incident to mind. What a lark! And what a funny little twerp 'Young Sparks' had seemed in those early days of their acquaintance. Yet, when they met again, some years later, in mid-Atlantic, he had shown more courage and endurance than chaps twice his age. You can never tell what will emerge in a moment of crisis, and certainly he had turned the tables on their early condescension and mockery. Together they had shared the blast of that ill-fated night – poor little blighter! A pity about Malabar Hill!

Richard had never enthused about the tropics, and the farther they went in an easterly direction, the stickier he became, while his natural energy and robustness dissolved rapidly in a state of lassitude it was difficult to shake off. The sun sapped his iron constitution, and drained him dry of that curious blend of authority and gentleness that made him so popular among the mixed company of men who shared his way of life. He had literally to flog himself, in the tropical heat, and only force of habit, combined with disciplinary action, saved his face on many occasions. He could readily understand how so many Englishmen, working 'out east', fell victim to the habit of drinking whiskies and soda at all hours of the day, for he felt the same need for a stimulant at the first hot breath of the east – usually at Port Said. But, in his own case, whisky didn't help, and its aftermath left only a sour taste in the mouth, and a resolve to stick to iced beer in future! But any strong resolve seemed doomed to failure once the cooling breezes of the Mediterranean were left behind, and, for a few weeks, till he could fill his panting lungs again with the cold tingling air of the western hemisphere, he usually took the line of least resistance. A polar bear, set down in the middle of the Sahara Desert, could not have felt more uncomfortable and out of his rightful element than Richard Seal, east of Suez!

His practical jokes became boorish, and his handsome face, so alert and eager in a Channel gale, wore a look of extreme distaste, or a faintly sardonic smile, intensely irritating to his confederates. His prowling walk would take on the guise of a stealthy cat. Hands in pockets, he assumed such an air of bored indifference, it was almost impossible to reach the man who had sailed with them from Liverpool less than three weeks earlier. Several of the crew, more especially those from 'over the Border', felt this same crippling lassitude in the tropical sun, but managed to maintain a small measure of their natural cheerfulness and humour.

But not Richard – it was all or nothing!

When he was bored or angry, or suffering from a hangover, everyone knew what he was suffering within the short space of half an hour! His symptoms were written on his face – 'Dick's in a bit of a stew' they would say, or, 'Who's upset the Third Mate, he looks like he could murder somebody!' But his popularity, instead of diminishing, seemed to increase as these human weaknesses became apparent – east of Suez. For it was generally assumed, by the lower orders, when he first joined the ship that he would be a very 'hard nut to crack' – and by his superior officers that 'he looked a bit of a so-and-so'. His arrogance, even in those days, supported the theory that 'young Seal was a cut above the rest'. But this noticeable characteristic had developed as he grew to manhood from a sense of injured pride and injustice.

Why were his parents killed in that car crash before he had time to know them? Why hadn't his maiden aunt legally adopted him when she could well afford to do so? Why did he have to pretend to a background he had never possessed – a family who had existed only in his imagination? In a Home swarming with children, you could be absorbed as one of the crowd – a nonentity. Or you could be a 'somebody' – and Richard Seal had decided, at the ripe age of eight, that he would be a somebody!

It must have been rather a relief to the Matron, and her overworked staff, when the maiden aunt provided the money to cover boarding school fees, for they wrongly supposed this particular little rebel would have to 'toe the line' once and for all. Fortunately for everyone, he soon developed an aptitude for sport, and all his energy and enthusiasm was quickly absorbed on the playing fields. Academically, he was backward, but this was not considered a calamity. To be included in the junior soccer team and cricket eleven, as well as being a fearless swimmer, was far more likely to meet the approval of the majority of the masters and pupils, and this early environment had shaped his character. Without parental affection and influence, some essential link is missing from the pattern of childhood. A hardness developed and a fighting spirit emerged from the small object of pity and charity an unkind fate had chosen to abandon.

5

The tedious hours pass slowly in a foreign port. Playing cards, drinking hot, strong tea, football pools and the wireless provided a few of the senior members with an excuse to stay aboard. This included the two stewardesses who suffered the same extremes of heat and cold as the men, but had no further desire to adventure beyond the close confines of their stuffy cabins. In twenty years of seafaring, they had 'seen everything and done everything'. There was nothing new under the sun, and they were as tough and indestructible as 'the Second' and 'Old Sparks'. They usually spent the few weeks of respite from seasick passengers and cheeky children laconically stitching torn sheets and recounting endless yarns, in a haze of tobacco smoke, with the inevitable teapot filled at regular intervals by the uncomplaining 'boy' whose duty it was to wait on them.

The stifling afternoons found them both asleep and snoring loudly, on their respective bunks – their plump figures draped expansively in florid oriental dressing-gowns, for which they had bargained, with malicious enjoyment in the street market of Singapore during the period when street markets and 'natives' were still a novelty. (A quarter of a century later, they would have been surprised and shocked, if they were still alive, to read in Richard Seal's autobiography, a single paragraph in which he referred to the 'two sex-starved females, of uncertain age'.)

Perhaps the young stewardess of the old *Braemar* mined in mid-Atlantic – if she had survived – would be equally surprised to find another paragraph, in a much later chapter, referring briefly, but kindly, to her embarrassing indisposition: 'Poor Liz, she looks quite ill, she will never make a stewardess. Andy has promised to keep an eye on her, and to let me know if the sickness continues.'

The Indian Ocean was no match for the Atlantic, in Richard Seal's opinion, but he could see for himself, on moonlit nights, that it held a kind of magic in its phosphorescent beauty. Flying fishes darted like dragonflies over the glistening water, and added to the sense of unreality, as though they came and went on wings of gauze at the touch of an unseen hand, and vanished like fairy creatures beneath the glossy surface of the sea. Richard would smile to himself, on the bridge, at these whimsical thoughts, for he was not very imaginative as a rule, and this kind of soft, evasive beauty hadn't the power to stir his senses, as a fierce Atlantic gale, or wild, lashing seas. Sunset and sunrise he always found exceedingly beautiful, but in moonlight, again because it held this elusive quality of the flying fishes, he found little excitement.

Yet his heart never failed to beat excitedly on the return voyage at the first glimpse of the Lizard. He could never emigrate, or settle in a foreign land, for this little corner of England would pull him back. He was not a Cornishman, but he would watch the land smudge the horizon with a lump in his throat, and tears in his eyes. This was the moment so many emigrants must wait for, he thought. But what were his emotions compared to theirs, who had waited for years, maybe a lifetime, for that first glimpse of England.

It always seemed to Richard that he had been away for a very long time, especially when they returned from the eastern hemisphere. So many impressions had filled his mind; so many changes of weather and climate, in a few short weeks.

They would sail from Liverpool in blue serge uniforms, on

frosty nights in mid-December, or creep through the fogs in February – muffled to the chin in great-coats and scarves, with their faces drenched in mist or sharpened by the frost. In less than three weeks, they would receive the order to change, and they would all emerge, like new men, in immaculate tropical uniform, as though they had stepped from Winter into Summer by merely changing their clothes! But with the new white uniform went a new personality, together with the tormenting certainty of a crippling lassitude – and sweat! Richard could change his shirt twice a day and plunge into a cold bath every time he came off watch, but still he would sweat!

There were beaches on the Malabar coast, shining white and mysterious in the moonlight, but the water lapping those beaches would be warm and sultry, lacking the sparkle and colour of other waters nearer home. Richard complained of its lukewarm, unrefreshing qualities, but his companions revelled in it. 'You're nuts!' they would tell him with yells of derisive laughter.

Richard was always aware of the beauty and strength in his own body. Modesty never prevented this natural admiration. Why should it? He looked and felt magnificent! It pleased and satisfied his ego to see the covetous glances of his companions as he stripped off his clothes.

The shy, admiring glances of the young stewardess did not escape him either, but he pretended indifference. His superb physique obviously impressed her, as he intended it should! Andy was following her around, and keeping a protective eye on her, he noticed. They were an odd looking pair going in to bathe – Liz so long and lanky, Andy short and sturdy.

'What's she like – any good?' Richard had questioned the Purser at dinner, one evening, during the first week out from Liverpool. It was the natural curiosity they all felt for a newcomer, on the staff, on her first voyage.

'As far as I'm concerned we could have left her ashore

for she hasn't completed a single stint of duty since we sailed,' grumbled Burton irritably. 'It reflects badly on my department and adds to the work of poor old Carter and Bond. Heaven knows, they've got enough to contend with already without a junior stewardess putting herself to bed every time the blasted boat rocks!'

'Poor kid,' Richard didn't envy her trying to please Burton and those two crabby old stewardesses, who resented the addition to the staff, and saw it as the first indication of a retirement both were dreading. The Purser was not very popular among his confederates, but the majority of passengers liked him. In his own department he was a strict disciplinarian; his abrupt manner and biting tongue could be very harsh to a sensitive new recruit. But naturally he was upset at any suggestion of inefficiency in his department. Richard could understand that, for Andy was a bit of an embarrassment on the bridge and he often had to cover up for him as he hadn't yet found his sea legs. But he was such a plucky little devil, you had to admire the way he staggered on watch in a howling gale, looking like a bit of washed-up flotsam! Andy had a spartan upbringing and would eventually make the grade, of that fact Richard was certain. But he was not so sure about Liz, whose middle-class background had been too genteel, for the rough and tumble of shipboard life. She had in fact been placed rather than appointed by recommendation or merit and Burton hadn't been consulted. And nobody had apparently inquired if Liz was a good sailor!

'She's no strong, the puir lass, and they are all down on her like a ton of bricks. A girl canna be expected to work when she's sick as a dog, mind you, she's no coward, and she does'na give in without a wee bit of a struggle. But she's no suited to the job, and that's the honest truth, Dick.' Andy had shaken his head sorrowfully and added, 'Liz is no match for those two crafty old bitches, she's too sensitive, too genteel.'

'Yes, it's her blasted gentility that upsets the old girls, for they're a couple of tough old birds, Andy, and this rough seafaring life has knocked any refinement they may have started with, thirty years ago.' Richard mused, 'Would you say Liz had a fifty-fifty chance of survival with that trio all set to shove her out at the earliest opportunity?'

'Aye, she has, for she's stubborn, and the sea's in her blood.'

That was a month or more ago and Liz had found her sea legs in calm waters, and worked like a trojan to compensate for the bad impression she had made on her superiors during the early stages of the voyage. Richard had caught an occasional glimpse of her, struggling down a long alleyway, bent under the heavy weight of an over-loaded tray. Once they had met face to face on the aft deck as he went on watch, and she had blushed shyly and dropped her eyes, after bidding him a quiet good night. He had noticed the pallor of her tired face, the dark shadowed eyes, and that air of withdrawal that kept her apart from the rest. Only Andy had penetrated her defences and that mainly because they had a mutual regard for their queezy stomachs! Here, on the Malabar coast, enjoying their off duty recreation, they were still inseparable. The more lively members of the crew had gone in search of female company with some sex-appeal. You couldn't get far with a girl who obviously preferred the company of the dogs on the boat deck! – as the cheeky young quartermaster had explained, quite candidly.

Beth was troubled as the weeks went by and she continued to read aloud the pages of typescript on which Richard Seal had spent so many arduous hours. It was good reporting, she decided, but it lacked that essential ingredient to a good story. He was more journalist than author. 'The Sea Was My Mistress' was nothing more than a journal or documentary – a man's impressions and recollections of his youth – a group of characters who never came to life under his pen. The material was there; the backcloth of the sea, sufficient to establish interest, but it was not enough. The theme was missing, and it lacked suspense and animation. She was troubled by her own unspoken criticism, for she hadn't intended to be critical.

Everything he did now was wonderful in her eyes. She admired and loved him, but she knew for certain he would never make a successful author, for his first brain-child seemed doomed to failure. As she watched his day-by-day determination to fill a certain number of pages, she felt the pangs of a fond mother, watching a child struggling with homework beyond the reach of its capacity. He saw everything with the clear-cut mind of a mathematician, rather than a creative artist. Lacking in imagination, he could only assemble facts and characters who moved and behaved like puppets, rather than real people. They lived in his mind and memory, but would not live on paper.

That was the tragedy.

Beth herself could make them live, for she felt she knew them all personally and intimately now – 'Old Sparks' and 'Young Sparks', 'The Second', 'Chips', 'Andy', 'The Old Man', 'Boy', 'Sandy' and 'Dusty'.

The young Richard Seal, as the hero of the story, would have been a much more colourful and romantic character if Beth had written the story!

Was he going to include the girl who became his wife, in a later chapter, she wondered? Would he change his mind and introduce a little feminine appeal?

He had told her, three months ago, it was a man's story, of a man's world, and women had no place in it. But she couldn't agree. Women may have passed like ships in the night on every voyage, but the young Richard Seal must surely have been aware of them, very conscious of their admiring glances as they walked the decks. In the Merchant

Navy, unlike the Royal Navy, there was no escape from the passengers en route. It was expected of the officers to help entertain the passengers in the evening, when they were off duty – to dance with unescorted ladies, and have a drink with lonely men. To be sociable, in fact.

What of the few privileged passengers who dined at the Captain's table in the company of the ship's officers every evening, over a four-course dinner? They would expect to be entertained. In the close confinement of a tourist-class vessel, with a passenger list of less than two hundred, the long sea voyage to the East or home to England could play havoc with the hearts of pretty girls and handsome young officers.

What would happen if this book was rejected by the publishers?

Would he accept defeat, or would he fight against it as bitterly and remorselessly as he fought separation from his wife? The truth must be faced. If Beth, who loved him, found the script disappointing, could the reactions of the publishers' readers be enthusiastic? Yet, for this short period of his life, everything revolved around himself as an author.

They were all closely involved now, and both Sheba and Beth had accepted the fact that they must play second fiddle to this all-important task, which absorbed every moment of his working day. Neither the woman nor the dog enjoyed the long hours of enforced silence, when a word or a bark would be frowned upon. But they endured it all for the sake of the man, as they endured his sudden rages, his sardonic smile, and the dark, shuttered mask of his face when he chose to exclude them both. Unconsciously, he expected and demanded all their loyalty and obedience to this strict routine he had adopted. The unwritten law – he must not be disturbed – was recognised by both.

Beth crept around silently, her big hands moving quietly about the chores. Doors were never banged, or coals dropped suddenly on the fire. Saucepans were handled carefully, and wooden spoons replaced the noisy metal ones for cooking. Sheba, stretched on the floor, would lift her head and yawn prodigiously as Laura passed by. They would exchange a searching glance, a small sigh of resignation. It was their only contact, but it served as a link between the one who could see, and the other who could not see. Sheba's uncanny understanding of human behaviour had recognised the symptoms in the housekeeper's pale, sensitive face, in the dark, sorrowful eyes, and the tremulous mouth.

It had happened before.

Women were strangely susceptible to her master! The early serenity of this new housekeeper had been much disturbed since Christmas. Some days she was so obviously distressed she went out to the garden holding a handkerchief to her mouth – and came back quite calm and composed. Sheba would glance anxiously from one to the other when this happened, and instinctively realise there was nothing between them. Those sad, imploring eyes of the woman held no power or persuasion over the man.

It was better so.

Sheba guarded her enviable and unique position jealously. She was satisfied no real contact had yet been made between these two, for they had not touched. Without this wonderful sense of touch, it was impossible to make contact with a blind person – Sheba had been taught. It was part of her early training, and she had never forgotten its importance. Hands and voice together make perfect contact, but the voice alone could not reach the senses. While this woman used only her quiet, controlled voice, there was no real danger. The danger was in her hands. They were big, strong, capable hands, for she was a big woman, and they had no difficulty, it seemed, with shaking mats, polishing floors or washing dishes, but were strangely inclined to tremble when pouring a cup of tea or coffee – or mending a hole in a sock.

There was danger, too, of another kind, at the kitchen sink, when her master's soiled shirt was pressed to the woman's lips, then plunged into the wash tub. If the kitchen door stood open, this impulsive gesture was not lost on Sheba, for she felt its gentle impact, and shivered, involuntarily. Nothing escaped her watchful eyes. She was more wary of this one particular woman than any of the others who had served them – because she was different. The difference was not only in her voice, her appearance, and her manner, but something more – an intangible, mysterious 'something' which baffled Sheba. She had not yet been able to trace its origin, though she had a feeling of awareness and curiosity at their very first meeting on the doorstep. It was partly resentment, for she had realised the intrusion of another female meant trouble – women invariably brought trouble to her master. But, surprisingly, after the first day, there had been no trouble, for this woman did none of the expected things when the man was angry, miserable or intolerant. She was soothing, not disturbing. Yet the danger was still there – in her *hands*, if they chanced to meet the hands of the other. A long quivering sigh escaped her huge, powerful body when the woman set a meal before the man, or a cup of coffee. She knew, from past experience, this was the moment of easy contact that invariably led to trouble, and she was glad and relieved from anxiety when her master kept his hands on his knees till the danger was past.

One Monday morning in early February, Beth discovered a cluster of snowdrops in Richard's garden, and her spirits were suddenly and miraculously uplifted by this first indication of an early Spring. She had wandered down the path to hang the washing on the clothes line she had tied across the patch of tufted grass at the bottom of the garden, and stopped dead, with the heavy clothes basket balanced on her hip, to gasp at the unexpected beauty and delicacy of these tiny, pure white flowers in the muddy garden. The sturdier aconites had been blooming since early January, but their curled petals had not opened in the bleak, wintry weather. Winter jasmine covered the south wall of the cottage. Thin branches tapped in the biting wind on the kitchen window, and sprays of yellow blossom in a blue jug decorated the high mantlepiece over the wide chimney.

'Do you object to flowers in the sitting-room?' she had asked Richard Seal one afternoon, when they were sharing the pot of coffee she always made after lunch.

'Not at all, providing you keep them out of my reach,' he answered, quite affably. But he was feeling in a good mood that day, and could afford to be a little more gracious to a housekeeper who not only made the best coffee he had ever tasted, but also the most delicious chocolate cake! Altogether, she was quite the most satisfactory housekeeper they'd had in years, he had decided – efficient, kind and quiet!

Judging by her voice and her nice manners, she seemed rather well-bred, he thought, but all kinds of people went out to work these days, so he was not particularly surprised to find a housekeeper with a 'refined' accent. It had amused him a little at first, but then he had accepted the fact that she was a 'lady' as he accepted everything now – with a mixture of curiosity and contempt. She suited him, and Sheba seemed to approve of her. That was all he asked of a housekeeper – 'lady' or otherwise!

He had known, instinctively, she was a gentle, not an aggressive woman, when she came for the interview that day, for her gentleness had touched the raw edge of his aggression, as she sat there, so quietly, in her wet, steaming clothes, saying nothing. So he was prepared to humour her a little, from time to time, when he felt in the mood!

'Winter jasmine?' he frowned, trying to remember it – and Beth had put a spray into his hands, to feel and recognise. It was strangely exciting, after so many years of lost contact with nature, to hold in his hands flowers from his own garden.

This new discovery, that he remembered winter jasmine, pleased him enormously. Screwing up his eyes, he had turned to Beth and grinned disarmingly.

'I can see it as clearly in my mind as I saw it in reality – thirty years ago! It grew all over the front porch of my aunt's cottage in Wiltshire. I spent Christmas there one year, and I was going through a phase of nature study – birds mostly, I remember, but trees and flowers and plant life intrigued me. This winter jasmine was the only flower I could find, naturally, in December – bright yellow flowers, like little stars? And no leaves – am I right?'

'Perfectly,' she assured him, smiling at his enthusiasm.

So yellow was still yellow? And he had a 'feeling' for plants and flowers. It was not very much to get excited about, but it was a beginning, she thought – and she *was* excited! After so many uneventful days and weeks, she felt tremendously reassured by this one small incident.

So, on this Monday morning, she quickly hung up the washing, and hurried back indoors – forgetting, with this new discovery, to lift the latch quietly, and to wait until he had finished the page of typescript before interrupting his chain of thought.

'I've just seen the first snowdrops! Isn't it wonderful!' she exclaimed – then stopped short, at the expression on his face. 'I . . . I beg your pardon.'

She was blushing like a silly schoolgirl caught in an act of folly. Sheba glanced curiously from one to the other, and sensed danger in her master's darkened face, and the woman's agitation. The atmosphere was charged with tension. *They were making contact!* Suddenly Richard smiled, and stood up.

"All right. Where are they? I want to see them!' he announced, and reached out a hand.

Sheba sat up quickly, her nose quivering with the scent of this new danger. Her limpid eyes followed the man's outstretched hand with a last desperate appeal. 'Don't touch her!' she warned him, and barked three times. But he completely ignored her and her warning signal, and walked straight for the open door, where the woman waited with a bright flush on her cheeks, and her eyes wide with surprise.

Their hands met and held.

Sheba slumped on the floor and buried her head in her paws. She heard their footsteps on the cobbled stones, and the man's voice, teasing. It was the beginning of TROUBLE!

'They are just here, at your feet; only a few inches from the trunk of this old pear tree,' said Beth, quietly. They both stooped, and their joined hands slid carefully over the wet grass till Richard's exploring fingers closed on a thin, fragile stem. There was no clumsiness in his touch, as his fingers travelled up the stem to the white petals. She marvelled at the lightness and deftness of his touch, for her own hands were clumsy. Crouching in the grass, she could watch the taut muscles of his lean face, his twitching brows, his hard mouth, and dark, intense eyes, while he carefully counted and examined the snowdrops. She was aware of her own racing pulses, and his calm detachment. Her eyes travelled over his face, and fastened on his stubborn chin.

'What a man!' she thought, with a sob in her throat, and stood up to move away from him, for the urge to gather his greying head to her breast was too strong.

'Thank you, Beth. Have you anything else to show me?' he was asking, as he stood beside her, but she was too overcome with emotion to answer.

Stretching his arms to the sky, his hand fastened on a branch, and he smiled reflectively.

'I was a great tree-climber, as a youngster. There wasn't a tree I couldn't climb within the wooded three acres of land surrounding that Children's Home. Had some nasty falls, though – this wrist has been broken twice, a leg fractured, and a collar-bone put out of action – can't think why I didn't break my blasted neck!' He laughed, then was suddenly serious. 'Do you know, Beth, I've just realised what went wrong with our marriage. If we'd had a child . . .' With a long drawn sigh he dropped his head on his arms, and stood there, remembering.

Sheba was coming down the path, with her tail between her legs, looking rather dejected.

Half jokingly, Beth told him, 'Sheba's coming to fetch you; she doesn't approve of all this gallivanting in working hours!'

He made no answer, and she left him standing there, wrapped in the folds of an irretrievable past, still as a statue, clutching the branch, with his head on his arms.

There was nothing she could do—her moment had passed, and she was back where she had always been, since she first set foot in this place.

Sheba went by, but did not glance up. The path was narrow, and Beth stepped aside, in the mud. The dog went on, whimpering like a child. Richard lifted his head, flung out his arms and called, 'Sheba! Come, girl!'

And the dog bounded forward and was caught in the grip of those two hands – hands that could close in a vice of steel, or touch the petals of a snowdrop with such delicate deftness.

Making the bed a few minutes later, Beth heard them come in, and then the rattle of the keys and the tinkling bell told her that Richard Seal was back at work. She hadn't realised she was crying till a tear trickled into the corner of her mouth. She was kneeling on the floor, turning over Richard's underwear in the bottom drawer, for she had washed his pyjamas, and he would need a clean pair for tonight. They felt a little damp, so she would have to air them on the clothes-horse in front of the fire. The hot water tank in the kitchen was still draped with damp towels. It was quite a problem in the Winter, this business of drying and airing. During the past few months, she had taught herself to be strictly methodical.

These pyjamas, for instance, when they were aired, must be tucked under the pillow, and no other place, or Richard would be turning the bed upside down, and cursing like a trooper later in the day. Every single thing had its proper place, and nothing must be moved. Only once had she fallen short of this important obligation, but she had phoned from the village call-box.

'I've left the coffee pot in the sink!' she told him breathlessly.

His chuckling laugh was reassuring on the other end of the line.

'I shall be getting my cards!' she added, flippantly, for she wouldn't dare to be flippant to his face.

'Can you hear the radio?'

'Yes.'

'I'm listening to "The Archers". I'm rather partial to old Walter Gabriel.'

'I'm sorry if I've interrupted.'

'Don't apologise, it's quite all right.' His voice was lazy and relaxed. She could picture him stretched out in the big armchair, with Sheba between his knees, and the firelight dancing on the walls.

'Goodnight.'

There was nothing else to say, for he wasn't really listening.

'Goodnight, Beth. Thanks for phoning.'

She had put down the receiver with a sense of disappointment. What had she expected?

She was holding the pyjamas to her wet face, quite unconsciously, when she felt a presence in the next room, and her body stiffened with fright. Sheba was blocking the open doorway between the two small bedrooms. Squatting on the floor, Beth hugged the pyjamas to her breast like a shield, and gazed, hypnotised, into those gleaming, yellow eyes. She could neither move nor speak.

Sheba growled, but did not move from the doorway.

'Sheba! What are you doing upstairs? Come down instantly!'

Richard's voice reached her, harsh with annoyance, from the bottom of the stairs. Sheba's eyes went limpid; her body quivered, then she turned away, and went slowly down the stairs.

Beth struggled to her feet. She could hear Richard scolding the dog severely.

'Who gave you permission to leave this room? Go and lie down! Bad girl! Are you all right, Beth?' he called out, anxiously, from below.

'Yes – I'm all right.'

'You don't sound very convincing. I'm coming up,' he announced. 'Has anything happened? Did Sheba . . .?'

'No.'

He sighed with relief.

'You mustn't let her bully you. She's a bit possessive at times,' he reminded her, not unkindly.

'Yes, she is,' Beth agreed.

'Well, that's the second interruption this morning. I seem to have lost the thread. Shall we have some coffee, then I'll make a fresh start?'

'I'll be down in a moment,' she said.

Coffee! If only he knew how badly she needed it! She was still trembling as she followed him down the stairs.

Sheba was stretched on the floor, in her usual place. The expression on her face was blandly innocent of anything but a mild curiosity in the housekeeper's rather large feet, as they went by! Then she lifted her head and yawned.

When Beth reached her own home that same afternoon, and was welcomed by Cindy and the pups – she thought there could hardly be a bigger contrast in their canine companions than Sheba and Cindy. It was good to come back to her, with her soft brown eyes, and the lively puppies, so full of fun and hischief. She hadn't a shoe they hadn't chewed, or a decent chair to sit on! What did it matter? Here she was her own mistress, and she liked a bit of a muddle. After the other, where everything had to be always in its proper place, it was a relief to scatter her own belongings, and to feel relaxed.

It had been a day of surprises – pleasant and unpleasant!

Putting a match to the sitting-room fire, she sat on the hearth rug, watching the puppies chasing their tails round the table, remembering her nervousness when Sheba had growled. She had always known the dog resented her, and always careful to treat her with cautious respect. After all, she wasn't just an ordinary dog. She was superb, in her way – highly intelligent and disciplined. It could have been a terrible, as well as a terrifying experience, if Sheba had not been so expertly trained and disciplined – and Richard's influence less strong. Surprisingly, Beth realised she was no longer afraid of the dog, for she was nearer to understanding its feelings than ever before.

Sheba was a bit jealous. It was natural. But she was also intelligent enough to sense danger. The years with Marion must have been both puzzling and disturbing to a dog like Sheba. Perhaps she was safeguarding herself, and her master, from any repetition of that unhappy period? Dogs have long memories – like elephants!

'Well, she needn't worry. Richard Seal is safe enough with me!' she thought, a little bitterly, as the sparks flew up the chimney.

6

The advertisement in the post office, and the local paper, had brought but a poor response. Only two of Cindy's puppies had been promised good homes, and a third with the neighbour's child, who looked after them during the day.

Sunday afternoons, since Christmas, had been allocated to this particular purpose, and Beth had stayed indoors to meet any callers who came to look at the pups. They were old enough now to leave their mother, and all were strong and healthy, but it seemed there was little enthusiasm in the modern home for young animals, with so many mothers out to work. The days were gone when almost every family naturally included a dog and a cat. Two children in the village had been promised a puppy, and had actually selected one, but had changed their minds later – or been persuaded by their mothers to change their minds. To be left with two puppies, as well as Cindy, was rather more than Beth could afford to keep. Besides, she had to earn a living, and could not travel around with three dogs! Neither could she afford to stay at home for more than three months of the year, even with the most careful budgeting. She had few qualifications and practically no ambition, but people liked her, and sent for her again and again when threatened by illness, old age, or a new baby!

'Beth is so kind and capable, and she doesn't fuss!' they said of her. It was better than nothing, but what had she done with her life, after all the money that was spent on her education?

So she waited, with some anxiety, on the last Sunday in February, for prospective buyers of dogs. The village seemed almost asleep on Sundays, these days, she noticed. In the Summer, families went off to the coast for the day, and seemed to hibernate in the Winter with their television sets. A few children crept out of Sunday School muffled in duffle coats and hoods, looking curiously apathetic. Several of the older generation passed by on their way to church or chapel, as she waited at the window, for the tolling of the five-minute bell, to cross the road and enter by the little lych gate, between two ancient yews. The familiar smells of that old church were pleasantly nostalgic – a mixture of mustiness and mildew, of seasoned wood and polished brass, hassocks and hymn books, with the faint lingering odour of bygone days. So many hands had handled the books, so many knees had knelt upon the hassocks. But now the empty pews were filled only with ghosts, and a few solitary men and women who still found their faith renewed by constant repetition of the age-old service, or because the habit of a lifetime could not be broken.

Beth, in the second category, was as dedicated to the regular attendance at morning matins as she was dedicated to early tea and Osborne biscuits! She went automatically to church on Sunday – any church, anywhere, from force of habit. In the years since the end of the war, and the end of her short married life, she had lost count of the number of churches she had attended during her travels. Some of the people she had visited had been a little surprised and piqued to find the Sunday joint in the oven and the housekeeper missing from her post – but had no reason to complain when lunch was still served at one o'clock. This compulsion to attend the morning service, no matter whether the church be situated across the street or a mile away, was typical of Beth. She was conservative in her ways, old-fashioned in her views, and clung, tenaciously, to custom. On rare occasions she found the service and the sermon quite inspiring, and her thoughts uplifted to a higher plane, but usually the 'atmosphere' faded with the first glimpse of the outside world, and she shed its faded familiar garment as she would shed an old coat. Perhaps the word best applied to this lifelong habit of going to church was comfort. It was comforting to continue in the old ways; the follow the pattern of childhood, and devoted Christian parents. In a changing world, it was comforting to cling to something unchanged. She had not joined the choir because she had no voice for singing – it was too soft, too quiet, to be effective. When Easter and Christmas filled the churches with enthusiastic congregations, she was delighted; and came away with the same sense of pleasure and enjoyment as some people would feel after a party, or an evening at the Rose and Crown.

Her enjoyment of life was simple, uncomplicated; her happiness in a few faithful friends, her canine companions, and the Cotswold countryside. She was content, almost complacent, in her quiet way of life, till the day she stood in the porch of Rose Cottage, and the door swung open to reveal a man and a dog, so strangely, unexpectedly, vital and vigorous, that they had found her weak and defenceless. Together they had robbed her of complacency and changed her contentment to restlessness, and vague, unsatisfied yearnings. She was no longer certain of anything, save this one undeniable fact – she loved this man with a deep intensity of feeling that was alien to her quiet nature.

Comfortably installed in her favourite chair, with Cindy on her lap, and the pups curled in a heap on the rug, Beth was happily reading Miss Read's *Village School* when a loud rap on the front door made them all jump with alarm.

'Ah, a customer at last!' she told Cindy, and opened the door to two young boys, whose faces were vaguely familiar.

'Hullo!' they said.

Then she remembered where she had seen them – in the church choir.

'Hullo.' She smiled and invited them in.

'We come about a dog,' said one, importantly, stuffing his hands in his pockets.

'Yes, that's right,' the other agreed.

The pups, by that time, had encircled the boys' legs, and they were laughing, patting, admiring, with Cindy in the background, glancing anxiously at her offspring but no longer able to control them.

'So you want to buy a puppy?' Beth prompted. 'Have you got your parents' permission?'

'Sure!' said the confident one, with a grin. 'But 'e wants one too, and 'is Mum can't make up 'er mind, see? So we thought if we could take one on approval, sort of . . . ?'

They were sitting on the floor, in the passage now, with puppies swarming all over them, licking their faces, and tugging at the loose buttons on their duffle coats.

'How old are you?' she asked.

'I'm ten and Keith's eight and three-quarters. We got the money, Missus, like you said in the advertisement. Ten shillings each,' explained the confident one, who answered to the name of Butch.

They both dived in their pockets, and fetched up a handful of silver coins, with the nonchalant air of men of the world.

'We been saving it, see; we want a dog more than anything, don't we, Keith?'

'Yes,' agreed Keith, rather breathlessly, battling with a couple of lively pups.

'Why do you want a dog?' asked Beth curiously.

The younger boy looked at the other. It was difficult to put into words.

'Well . . .' Butch gave the question his serious consideration. 'There's nothing to do, not really, when you 'ave to take a walk, by yerself. But when you got a dog, well, it's smashing! See? And when Keith and me both 'ave dogs, well, can't you see it's going to be smashing?'

'Yes, I can,' she agreed. 'Fun for you and for the dogs! All right, you may have them, on condition that you promise to bring one back if Keith's mother objects to keeping it. I shall refund the money, and find another home for the puppy.'

'She won't object,' Butch declared stoutly. 'She promised 'im a dog, see? Only she couldn't make up 'er mind whether to 'ave a big one or a little un. Keith wants a little un, so it's sort of settled if 'e takes one of them.'

'You can't choose, I'm afraid,' Beth reminded them. 'These three are all promised, and will be collected this week. That leaves only this one with the brown patch on its face and this one, with the white chest.'

'We don't mind, they'll do,' Butch agreed, magnanimously, and immediately claimed 'brown patch'.

Keith seemed equally pleased with the other, for he was an agreeable small boy, with a peaked face and wistful smile. But she liked them both and felt she could trust them to be kind to the pups.

They went away, very conscious of themselves as the proud owners, with the puppies cuddled in their arms. Cindy ran after them, barking anxiously, then came back looking very sorry for herself.

'The time has come to let them go, my dear, they don't need you any more,' said Beth gently, as she closed the door.

On that last Sunday in February, Richard's mind refused to function according to plan and purpose, and the waste-paper basket overflowed on to the floor with screwed pages of typescript. Why wasn't Beth here to sort it out, and why hadn't he borrowed a tape-recorder from St Dunstan's, in the first place, when he started on this autobiography? Without a housekeeper to read back the typescript, memory could play false tricks. His irritation mounted as the morning hours ticked away, and his mind's eye refused to focus on the battle of the Atlantic. No amount of concentration would produce the picture he wanted to see and feel and remember.

Memory was blank; all those far-away yesterdays, lost in a nagging doubt of the present.

What had happened between Beth and Sheba?

Something had happened. Beth had lied to spare the dog. He knew she was lying, for he could feel the vibrations of her smothered distress, when he stood in the doorway. And he could detect the fear in her voice.

Sheba, surprised by his voice, in what was normally considered a silent period, got up to investigate.

Richard's spread hands invited her to come closer, so she slid between his knees, and licked his cold cheek with her wet, warm tongue. The irritation he had shown all morning completely vanished. His dark, frowning brows smoothed out. A tender little smile played over his face, and softened his stern features, while he fondled her head and ears, then her gaping jaws.

'You mustn't take any notice, my beauty. It makes no difference to you and me. Do you understand? *Absolutely no difference.* There is no need to be jealous of Beth – Beth is not Marion. You had every right to be jealous of Marion. Beth will give, not take from us. She doesn't want to separate us. That's where you are wrong – but I'm not yet sure how much she can endure, for our sakes! Still waters run deep! I'm a selfish brute, and I don't want to lose her. I'm not in love with her – but there is something about her that's rather endearing, almost familiar, in the sense that I feel at ease with her. Are you listening, girl?'

Sheba swished her tail emphatically, and barked twice. Richard laughed, as he took her forepaws on to his knees.

'All right, you are listening, and you are trying to understand – good girl! It's a little complicated, I agree, since I've told you so many times since the divorce that I have finished with women. Never again! – I swore to you, didn't I? Well, I was curious; Beth is so – so remote, and secretive, and my curiosity got the better of me. The snowdrops were just an excuse to take her hand, and walk down the garden with her. I wanted to see if her self-control would stand the test! Yes, I'm a brute. Well, it did, but I wish it hadn't, for I'm like a bear with a sore head today! It's disturbing to hold a woman's hand again, and feel something stirring you thought was dead. What do I want of her? Last night, for the first time, it was Beth, not Marion, in my thoughts, when I lay awake. But it was strangely soothing to think of Beth, and God knows I need soothing! Perhaps it's her secret weapon? I could almost believe, at this moment, it would be the answer to our problems. The future would be safe and secure. We could sit back comfortably and let Beth take over.

'But it wouldn't last, Sheba girl. We should be bored and restless, wrapped in security. No, if I can get this blasted book finished, we can be free and independent again. Where shall we go? What shall we do? Who cares! Something will turn up. It must be the Spring making me feel so restless again. It couldn't be Beth, could it? No, it's more likely to be Andy back from Singapore, blast him! I wonder where he goes next? God! How I envy him!

'Sheba, I've got to get out of here! I can't sit here any longer today, or I shall go mad. Let's play truant! Let's not bother to get our dinner. We can have a glass of cider and a beef sandwich at The Crown, and then walk over the hill to Lovington. It's only two or three miles each way. How's that for an idea? Get your harness then. Go on! Get your harness. I know it's the wrong time of the day to take a walk, but don't bully me!'

Sheba was mystified, but, as always, she obeyed his command, and brought the white harness. When she saw he was putting on his overcoat she was finally convinced, and entered into his mood with great excitement.

They went out boldly, slamming the door behind them, and swung down the lane, matching their long steps with eager anticipation.

It was only the third time Richard had called at The Crown for a drink, but he was hailed like a long-lost associate as he stood on the threshold with Sheba.

'Why, look who's here!'

'It's Mr Seal and Sheba!' greeted them from all directions.

A fire roared up the chimney. It was hot and smoky, friendly and cheerful. The smell of beer and strong tobacco predominated – somebody was smoking a foul old pipe!

Richard coughed and grinned amiably, while they made room for him at the bar. Helpful hands guided him, and he could feel the stir they had caused in the Sunday morning assembly of regulars. Sheba was admired, but they kept their distance, for she wasn't a dog you took liberties with, and she had the manner and appearance of a well-trained police dog, in that crowded little pub.

'It's nice to see you, Sir. We wondered when you would be looking in again.'

The landlord, leaning on the counter, looked into a pair of dark, penetrating eyes, and shivered. It was uncanny. This chap's eyes were brighter than those who could see – made you feel uncomfortable.

'What will you have, Sir?'

'It's on me,' said a pleasant voice at his elbow.

'Thanks very much – cider, please! Oh, and Harry – I'd

like a round of your very good beef sandwiches. I've had no dinner.'

'You've got a jolly good memory, Sir. Why, it must be three months or more since you were here?'

Richard laughed indulgently. 'If my memory stretched no farther than three months, Harry, I should be in a bit of a mess with this book I'm writing!'

'Yes, I see what you mean, Sir. How's it going – that book of yours?'

'Very well indeed, thanks.'

Not for the world would he have confessed to anything other than perfect co-ordination and success in this new venture.

Surrounded by the customers, he felt a glow of importance and superiority. They admired and respected him. He could feel it in their presence; hear it in their voices. The landlord had told him, that first time he called in for a drink, that it was a pleasure to serve him, for he'd never had a blind gentleman in the place before – or seen a guide dog.

'It's on the house, Sir,' he had insisted, when Richard pulled out a handful of coins.

It was always the same – nobody would accept any payment! And they hung on his words as though he were uttering the most profound truths! Amusing really – when it wasn't so damn irritating. The pair of them, he and Sheba, seemed to hold almost the same attraction for people as a barrel-organ and a monkey, or a performing bear at the circus. Every clever trick was applauded!

Well, he would give them good value. Draining the cider, he told them laconically, 'We are on our way to Lovington.'

The gasp of surprise was rewarding enough.

'Lovington?'

'Just you and that dog?'

'But it's nearly three miles!'

'Christ!'

Richard laughed carelessly, and finished the sandwiches. Sheba sat beside him, alert, attentive. She accepted the morsel of beef with grateful surprise. It was going to be a day of surprises, apparently.

'Well, Harry, what do I owe you?'

'It's on the house, Sir. It's a pleasure.'

'Thanks, Harry.'

He accepted it as his reward for entertaining the customers!

'Take care!'

'Mind how you go!'

'Don't get lost!'

And again, that single, astonished '*Christ*!'

'Cheerio!' they called after him.

'Cheerio!' he echoed, as he reached for the harness, and walked out with swaggering importance.

7

Several cars were parked in the yard, but Sheba steered easily and carefully between them, paused at the kerb to listen for traffic, and Richard's curt – 'Forward' – then with calm assurance, they both marched quickly across the road, and entered the lane directly opposite.

'I'll bet they are all peering out of the windows at The Crown,' thought Richard, mischievously. 'They don't believe we can do it; they think it's impossible – nothing is impossible! We must keep going due east, and that shouldn't be too difficult, with the wind in our faces.

It was so exhilarating; good for the liver and the morale. They were getting soft and pampered with Beth fussing over them, and waiting on them hand and foot, six days a week. Any sort of danger was preferable to sitting around on their backsides, playing safe. Sheba was his eyes. He had the most implicit faith in her guidance.

So he felt relaxed and confident, yet, at the same time, excited by this new experience. Refreshed by the cider and the beef sandwiches – Harry had been generous with that beef – Richard lifted his head and squared his shoulders. There was no hesitation in his firm step, no fumbling for a sure foothold as the lane narrowed and roughened. If he tripped, he wouldn't give a damn! If they lost their way, they would find it again. It was as simple as that. They had all the rest of Sunday, anyway, providing they were back by ten o'clock on Monday morning. Beth would be sending out a search party if they were missing! Would she believe they had actually walked to Lovington and back? She seemed to think it was marvellous just to walk to the village – a distance of only two miles, and a familiar road – easy! Poor Beth! If she thought to tame them with her gentle ways, she was sadly mistaken. They must be free and independent, or life was not worth living.

To walk alone, as they were doing now, with the wind singing in his ears, and the harsh cries of wild duck flying in from the Severn estuary. This was living! In spite of the snowdrops and Beth's prediction of an early Spring, there was still no sign of it in the elements. It was cold enough for snow.

Sheba had suddenly swerved, and they had missed a tree by a small margin. He could sense its bulk.

'Good girl!' he encouraged.

'I could have split my head open on that,' he thought, but kept the thought to himself. It was unwise and unkind to disturb her attention outdoors, when she was wearing the white harness. She was on duty. It was not a time for confidences or conversation.

There is a time for everything under heaven.

He remembered reading that, but where, and when?

The Bible? . . . Could be.

A time to love and a time to hate,

A time to laugh, and a time to weep,

A time to embrace, and a time to refrain from embracing...

No, it didn't sound exactly biblical, with that bit about embracing. But he had no memory for quotations, or their origins.

A time to embrace and a time to refrain from embracing.

That was strangely appropriate, anyway!

They were climbing quite a steep hill now, and when they reached the summit, he had a wonderful sensation of space and freedom. Sheba was panting, so he gave the order to sit, but she was soon fretting to be on her way – a little anxious, naturally, on the unfamiliar route, and so very conscious of her great responsibility.

They must have covered another half mile when she pulled up abruptly, quivering with fear. And Richard instantly planted both feet firmly on the ground.

A man's voice called urgently in the distance 'Stand still! – for God's sake!'

A moment later, he ran up from behind, grasped Richard's arm and explained breathlessly, 'It's an old gravel pit. Very dangerous. God, but you gave me a fright. I thought you were going over the edge. That's a wonderful dog you've got there.'

Richard was trembling now, for fear is contagious, but he managed to hide his nervousness.

'Do you smoke?' he asked the stranger almost casually, offering his cigarette case.

'Thanks, I could do with one.'

'So could I,' said Richard, deftly flicking a lighter.

'Where are you making for?'

'Lovington.'

'Lovington? Well, you've come about half a mile off your track. It's easy enough. I did it myself the first time I came this way. I'll walk back with you, and put you right.'

'Thanks very much. That's very decent of you.'

They retraced their steps in silence, after they had commented on the weather. Richard had never acquired the easy habit of talking to strangers, and this man had nothing to say. Perhaps he was still a little unnerved or struck dumb by Sheba's cleverness.

'Well, this is the place and here's the path. Just carry on over the next hill and straight down into the valley. You're about halfway at this point.'

Richard thanked him again, and they went their separate ways.

Sheba hadn't cared much for that chap, and she was still suffering from the shock of the gravel pit. He gave the command 'Forward!' She would be all right now they were alone, and she could concentrate all her attention on the route.

Funny girl – but the best friend a man ever had. They had given each other such confidence and assurance that nothing seemed impossible now. Their reactions were so spontaneous it seemed uncanny to sighted people. A sort of current sped between them, but it was difficult to explain. In that split second that Sheba had stopped dead on the brink of the gravel pit, her warning signal had reached him, and the sensation of a yawning space beneath his feet was very real indeed – in the pit of his stomach. They had never grown careless of each other, or this wonderful harmony that existed between them. And they had not aged either. Sheba had put on a little weight, and he supposed he had a few grey hairs, but that was natural. His body was lean and strong and healthy. Yes, they were tough as steel, the pair of them. When the book was finished, they would be ready to conquer new worlds. It was getting to be a bit of a bore, but he had to finish it, for it was against his principles to leave a job unfinished. What a test of endurance, though – seven days a week!

He wondered what Beth thought of it – his first, and last, brain-child!

There would never be another, for he was much too active by nature. She had, as yet, made no comment, or passed any opinion on it. But then, he hadn't asked for it, and his pride prevented him. It would be too humiliating to be criticised by a woman. No, he would take a chance with that publishing chap, and if he turned it down, it wouldn't be too disastrous after all. On this glorious hill, alone with Sheba, he could even face the possibility that it might be refused publication, and he had wasted a whole year!

Within the walls of a house, every issue seemed to acquire such exaggerated importance. To clear his mind, to open his heart, to face reality, and to resolve never to lose his identity – he must have the sky for a roof, and the wide open spaces.

Sheba had completely regained her confidence now that they were on the right track. It was a most enjoyable walk, and they must do it again. Next time he must remember to put a bar of chocolate in his pocket, for such invigorating air whetted the appetite. What wouldn't he give for a slice of Beth's chocolate cake at Lovington!

Now they were walking on grass – now they were climbing a gate – now they were actually in Lovington, for a single church bell was tolling solemnly. It couldn't be a funeral on Sunday afternoon, so it must be a christening, he decided, remembering the one he had attended, with Marion, some years ago. In which case there would be a few people around. What a lark if he got himself invited to the christening tea! He would turn on the charm, and smile pleasantly. It might work! After all, they were quite a distinguished-looking pair, so it had been said. And he could count on Sheba to be looking her best, now that she was relieved of anxiety.

'Clever girl!' His hand patted her broad back, and she lifted her head proudly, panting with relief and pleasure. She knew she had pleased him, and that he was feeling happier than for some time past. But she was still on duty, and certain precautions had to be taken in these strange surroundings.

Cars were gathering on the kerb, people collecting in a group, children running in circles, and men with cameras, blocking the path. It was all rather confusing after the long, lonely trek over the hills, and the deep, quiet valley.

Sheba halted, and waited patiently, but nothing happened. Well, somebody had to move! They had a right to the pavement, and they must assert their right! Her indignation mounted. It was humiliating to be ignored. She barked, once. It was enough to startle them!

The cameras dropped, the children stood gaping, and the

crowd pushed back to the churchyard wall. The silence was impressive. Sheba was satisfied.

'Excuse me, am I interrupting something important?'

Her master's voice was pleasing and polite.

'No, not at all. It's just the baby's christening,' a woman's voice answered nervously.

'Can we help you?' asked another.

The baby yelled, and somebody told it to hush.

'Is there a café in this village? I wondered if I could get tea?' asked Richard, with an innocent smile on his handsome face.

'Yes, there is a caff, but it's closed on Sunday,' volunteered a bright young person in a scarlet coat.

'What a shame,' murmured several grey-haired matrons, looking at the pair with real concern.

'We've walked over from The Crown,' Richard pointed out, carelessly.

A ripple of amazement swept over the group.

'Gosh!' exclaimed the bright young person at his elbow, and Richard turned his smile on her.

She was whispering to her mother. They were all whispering, but he could hear every word!

'You can't possibly walk all that way back without a cup of tea,' decided the baby's godmother. 'Now, if you would like to sit in the church porch, it won't take more than half an hour. Then someone will walk back with you to Colin's place. It's not far. I'm sure you will be most welcome,' she added graciously.

And several voices echoed, 'Yes, most welcome.'

Richard bowed. 'Well, that's exceedingly kind of you. Thank you very much indeed.'

'I'll look after him,' a young boy's voice insisted, importantly.

'No, I will!' contradicted a small girl.

'Now don't fight over him, children; you can *both* look after him!' the baby's godmother decided.

The baby, who seemed to have been completely forgotten, yelled again.

'Let me take her,' said the bright young person, surprisingly.

And all was quiet.

Several children had collected, and they swarmed about him.

Sheba was the big attraction, of course. The baby would play second fiddle with these youngsters. Richard explained that Sheba was on duty in the white harness. They were buzzing with excitement, for the boys had already decided the christening part of the ceremony was going to be a bit of a bore, anyway, and they were really only interested in the tea party that followed.

Families and friends trooped into the church. Richard, Sheba, and the children walked behind. There was another little scuffle inside, however, for now the children had decided they would sit in the porch with Sheba, and had to be persuaded by several male members of the family to 'behave themselves'.

Reluctantly they followed their elders.

'Don't go away, mister!' whispered a young boy, urgently.

'Don't worry, old chap, I won't move,' promised Richard, with an engaging grin.

Phew! What a commotion! But rather exciting. They seemed a nice friendly crowd, and the children were so frank and amusing. It was good to sit quietly for a while before the next hubbub broke loose! Sheba was obviously puzzled and confused by these strange manoeuvres. She stood between his knees, a bit hesitant.

'It's all right, girl – relax,' he told her, gently.

They sat there together, listening to the strains of the organ, and the voices raised in a well-known hymn . . .

There's a Friend for little children
Above the bright blue sky . . .

Memory touched his wandering thoughts, and he was back

in Sunday School, with Mick Frazer, Barney King and Bobby Giles. What a bunch of young devils! Talk about juvenile delinquents – and he was the leader. There was never any doubt about that. He smiled at the memory.

There's a home for little children
Above the bright blue sky . . .

Well, he hoped it would be an improvement on the other Home, or it would be a bit overcrowded? Nick had been up there for years. Only ten, and snuffed out like a candle, with meningitis – poor little devil. But Nick with a harp? Never! Somebody would have to take him in hand, or he would be up to all sorts of tricks with St Peter, and the rest! Was he still a boy of ten, or was he living again in another body? Reincarnation seemed much more feasible than a bright eternal heaven beyond the sky.

But it was all a profound mystery. God was the supreme monarch of the sea, the sky, the wind and the sun. This undeniable truth was made manifest to every seafaring man at the mercy of the elements.

But he was a stern God.

To be made the victim of an undeserved life penalty of blindness. Why? Why? There was no answer. Nobody had ever been able to answer that question. The Chaplain had tried, but failed to explain the significance of a loving and merciful God, and total blindness at twenty-five?

A sudden piercing yell from within the church jerked him back to the present, and he shook off the past with a sense of relief. Why did he allow himself to be so disturbed by the past, when bitterness had proved a stumbling block both in his marriage, and his personal friendships. Only Andy could put up with him.

Well, this infant was certainly making its mark on its first big occasion!

'Here we are, mister,' said a voice at his elbow.

'Gosh! It took a long time to christen that baby!'

Once more he was surrounded, and they all seemed to be talking at once.

'Mum said I could take him.'

'No, *me*!'

They were at it again!

'Listen all of you!' They stopped instantly, and he knew he had their attention. 'If you lead the way, Sheba will follow, and I follow Sheba. Is that understood?'

'Yes!'

He laughed, and they set out like the Pied Piper in reverse!

He could hear the parents, aunts, uncles and godmothers chattering excitedly about the baby's behaviour.

'Wasn't it awful to yell like that when the Vicar was holding her no nicely?'

'I went hot all over!'

'Well, it's supposed to be lucky if the baby cries!'

'Thank God that's over! – that must be the infant's father?

'You all right with all these kids?' asked the bright young person.

'Fine, thanks.' He was almost one of the family, now!

'Come on, then!' shouted the boy impatiently, from the front rank.

The girl giggled. 'Isn't it a scream – a sort of body-guard? If you could see them . . .' Then she stopped short with a little gasp of embarrassment. 'I'm sorry – I didn't mean . . .'

And that was the last he heard of her.

'Forward!' he told Sheba.

'Forward!' echoed the children, clearing the path as they went along.

'But I don't want to walk in the street,' protested an unfortunate child coming in the opposite direction.

Richard supposed she had been unceremoniously pushed off the pavement.

Cars were passing, the drivers hooting and calling out

encouragement. Quite a disturbing Sunday afternoon for the peaceful citizens of Lovington!

Now they had stopped at a house in the main street – now they were being pushed inside – now they were tripping over chairs and children – and he was being explained to the hostess.

'Do sit down. Make yourself at home,' said a brisk voice, cheerfully, and he was steered to a low settee. Putting Sheba between his legs he quickly assured her, and he sat there, tingling in every nerve, while the guests poured into the room, and filled the house with excited chattering. It was bedlam! Then, at last, the rattle of tea cups, and somebody put a cup of tea in his hands, and a plate on his knee.

'Please, may I have some water for my dog?' he asked.

'I'll get it!'

'No – me!'

Another little scuffle among the children, and a soft placating voice, 'Now, children, don't fight.'

He discovered his plate contained a variety of savoury bridge rolls, and a generous slice of iced cake.

The children were quiet now, and busy with their tea. A buzz of voices reached him from the far end of the room.

'It must be one of those big, double rooms, part dining and part sitting-room,' he thought. 'There would be a television set in the corner.' The glare of an electric fire scorched his face. He was still wearing his overcoat! It was hot and suffocating. He felt again the old sensation he had known in the flat, when Marion had filled the place with her friends, closed all the windows, and switched on all the fires.

He stood up, smiling apologetically. 'If you will excuse me, I must be getting back.'

His resonant voice dropped like a pebble in a pool. Nobody answered. Chairs were pushed back, and the children swarmed round him. Somebody took the crockery from his hand, and, amid the uproar, he paid his grateful compliments.

'The children will see you to the end of the road,' he was told, and a man's voice called after them, 'Are you sure you wouldn't like me to run you back in the car?'

'No, thanks – we shall manage!'

Once more the convoy set out, and spilled over the pavement. At the end of the village he climbed over the gate with Sheba, and turned to smile and wave 'Goodbye!'

'Goodbye!'

He could hear them scrambling on the gate, and their voices floated after him as he climbed the hill. They were still calling when he plunged into the quiet valley.

Away to the west, he could hear the faint, but unmistakable cries of the wild duck. A fox barked in the distance. The tingling air was cold and stung his face, and he lifted his head to breathe great draughts in to his panting lungs; then reached for a cigarette. Suddenly he shouted with laughter – in the pocket of his overcoat, wrapped in tissue paper, he discovered another slice of cake, and two little sandwiches – smelling strongly of fish paste!

The return journey presented no difficulties for Sheba was sure-footed and confident of her right path, and Richard certain they were heading due west. They stepped out boldly without fear or hesitation. The man and the dog, with the long strides and dark, proud looks had a primitive beauty on that lonely heath. They seemed to belong only to themselves – free, independent, untamed. They matched each other perfectly. The understanding and harmony between them had never been more close.

Then they trod, at last, the familiar path leading to their own cottage, pushed open the door and went in.

'We've done it!' Richard shouted, exultantly. 'Sheba, my beauty, we've done it!'

Removing the white harness, and his own overcoat, he dropped to his knees and embraced her. Tears pricked his eyes, and his throat contracted. Emotion flooded his heart. Together they had conquered another little world, climbed another little mountain. They had known the 'glory and the ecstasy' of travellers and explorers; felt the same exhilaration and the same unfettered joy in being alive. There was nothing they couldn't do together! Nothing impossible, or too difficult to attempt! But they must have faith in themselves. They were alone – they would always be alone, and fundamentally lonely. It was inevitable. But today had proved, once again, their determination to hold fast to those principles on which their relationship was founded – complete trust, loyalty and courage.

Free of the white harness, Sheba was quivering with joy and excitement – licking his face and flicking her tail. She was so pleased with herself! Her paws hung over his shoulders, like two arms about his neck.

The door stood wide open, and an owl hooted in the field adjoining the cottage. The wind had dropped, and it was very still and quiet. He wondered who would be living here next year, when Winter slid into Spring. Snowdrops? He had a sudden urge to find out if they were still there, under the old pear tree, and went down the garden with Sheba at his heels. She was surprised to discover him on his knees, crawling on the grass – but the day had been full of surprises! Yes, they were still there – beautifully and miraculously intact. His fingers closed on the drooping petals, on their thin, thread-like stems. He remembered the pleasure it had given Beth – this small discovery. She had lost her shyness and reserve, and had actually taken his hand – an unprecedented gesture!

Her gentle presence seemed to be rooted here, in this peaceful garden. It was very soothing, for now he was suddenly tired by the events of the day, and the strong, emotional climax. Scrambling to his feet, he stood there, leaning against the solid trunk of the old tree – remembering her.

Could one have both? Beth *and* Sheba? Liberty *and* Love?

Profound thoughts had occupied his mind most of the day. He could see everything with such clear perception – feel everything with all his senses, today. He was so extraordinarily alive! – or he had been, until a few moments ago.

Now, at the end of an exciting and eventful day, he realised he was quite exhausted, mentally and physically. But the satisfaction remained, and the conviction that it was right and necessary to continue the practice of self-discipline and self-determination. Yet now he felt that he wanted praise and appreciation, other than Sheba's – a weak spot in his armour?

With some reluctance, he recognised it was a *human* voice he was reaching for, in this quiet garden, with a desperate sort of yearning. *Human* arms about his neck and a *human* mouth to kiss.

But this was ridiculous!

'It's just the reaction,' he thought. 'I always feel this way when I've reached for the stars.' But it was more pressing and urgent today.

Beth *and* Sheba? Liberty *and* Love?

What a question! He sighed heavily, and was tortured by indecision.

No! He could never go through with all that again, passion turned to pity.

Sheba was standing still as a statue, a yard away. He could hear her panting breath. She knew he was disturbed by this new current of thought, that had trespassed unwittingly on their happy companionship, and she would be puzzled, growing suspicious of his sudden withdrawal.

With a supreme effort, he roused himself from reverie, pushed away the yearning for a human voice and human touch, and shouted 'Sheba, girl! I'm starving!'

Then they went indoors to cook the supper and make fresh coffee.

'Sausages and baked beans for me, but first I must get

your supper, girl!' he told Sheba, with forced gaiety, opening a large tin of her favourite dog food. She was lapping thirstily at the bowl of water, while he filled the food bowl with meat and hard biscuits. She liked her food dry, and he himself had the same preference. Gravies and sauces were messy! The sausages seemed to burn very quickly tonight, the beans stuck to the pan, and coffee boiled over. He was too impatient!

Then he stepped on a spot of grease and skidded awkwardly, to hit his head a shattering blow on the wall. 'Blast!' he yelped, and reached for the floor cloth. It was missing from its usual place on the hook beside the boiler. He had probably used it this morning to mop up something and forgotten to put it back. Beth always left everything in its proper place, and he never had to hunt for things.

Well, he must tread carefully in the meantime. Tomorrow she would be back. Tomorrow, at half-past eight, he would be listening for her step. She was always early these days – came early and left late. Perhaps she thought he hadn't noticed? He ought to pay her more. But he had a feeling she would be upset if they discussed the question of wages. After all. Beth wasn't just an ordinary housekeeper. She was rather special.

He ate a little of the burnt sausage and beans, but had no appetite. His head was throbbing painfully now, and he could feel the swelling over his right eye. Again he wanted the human touch, the human voice, commiserating. The gentle touch, the soft voice – Beth?

He would leave all the mess in the kitchen, and the washing-up, then tender his apologies in the morning. She wouldn't mind, she was so very amiable and kind. A nice-natured person – Beth.

As he stretched in the armchair, with his feet on the fender, he tried to imagine his throbbing head on her breast, and her big, cool hands on his bruised forehead.

It was very soothing, the thought and the expectation.

The phone rang suddenly and demandingly.

Now who could that be?

He lifted the receiver, and the voice in his thoughts was close to his ear.

'Mr Seal? Oh, I've been trying to get you all the evening. I'm so sorry, but I shan't be in tomorrow. Cindy was knocked down by a car this afternoon, and the vet doesn't hold out much hope. I can't think how she got out, but apparently she was looking for the two pups I had handed over to two young boys in the village . . .'

'I'm sorry.'

'Thank you.'

Before he could say another word, she had hung up the receiver.

She was crying.

8

The second rap on the knocker that Sunday afternoon was even more urgent than the first.

The boys, still hugging the pups, were on the doorstep again, with pale, scared faces.

'Your dog – a car just knocked it down!' blurted out the elder; and the younger boy began to cry.

'Where is she?' Beth asked quietly, with a little shiver of pain in her heart.

'In the ditch. It crawled there after it was 'it by the car, see? The car didn't stop, neither,' the boy explained, breathlessly. 'It wasn't our fault, 'onest! We never saw the dog following us, did we, Keith?'

'No, we never saw nothing!' sobbed Keith, miserably.

'It's all right, don't cry. It's not your fault.'

Beth hugged the small shoulders, as they hurried down the road.

By four o'clock on Sunday afternoon in the winter, the village was deserted. Tea and television attracted most people home early these days. A hundred yards or so from home, Cindy lay on her back in the ditch, pitifully helpless, and shivering with shock and pain. Her mild, brown eyes gazed up in mute appeal as they gathered round her.

'Poor Cindy, poor little girl,' Beth murmured, gently examining the small, shaggy body.

There was no sign of injury on her head or her legs, and no blood, but she whimpered like a hurt child at every touch of those gentle hands on her body. Internal injuries were much more serious than superficial ones, Beth thought wretchedly, as she gathered the dog in her arms.

Both boys were crying now, and the pups whining to get to their mother. Cindy's eyes widened with anxiety for a moment, then filmed again.

'Is she going to die?' a small voice asked, tearfully.

Beth looked down at them with a wan smile. 'I don't think so,' she said kindly. 'Now, don't you two worry any more about it. Run along home with the puppies, or they will be getting cold.'

'Okay.'

They were glad to get away.

The road was deserted, and she carried Cindy home. Wrapped in a rug, she laid her tenderly on the couch, shut the three remaining pups in the kitchen, and went out to phone the vet from the call box.

He had just got back from delivering a calf, but he was very sympathetic, and promised to be there in half an hour. She hurried back to Cindy. Would she still be alive? It had happened so suddenly, she was feeling quite stunned.

Cindy had not moved, but she was still whimpering. Beth knelt on the floor, stroking her head, and her soft, floppy ears.

'Poor darling – I wish I could do something.'

Her eyes were wet, her heart aching with pity. In all the years she had enjoyed the love and companionship of dogs, this had never happened before. They had all died peacefully of old age, and this sudden violent end to her gentle little Cindy was heart-breaking.

When the vet walked in, she was still kneeling there, but he barely glanced at her suffering face. He was concerned only with the poor little creature on the couch. His practised hands soon discovered the injury, and he gave her an injection. Only when he had finished could he spare a thought for the woman. She looked quite stricken, he thought, but then he remembered she was one of those women who really doted on dogs. He could hear the puppies barking frantically to be let out. They couldn't have come at a better time to keep her mind off this. (But they were all promised to new homes.)

'Well, my dear, that's all I can do for this poor little lady,' he said, kindly. 'I'll look in again in the morning.'

'Thank you,' she whispered.

He went out, closing the door softly.

It always seemed a pity that a woman like that had no children. She would have made a wonderful mother. She was all maternal, he thought. And he went back to his tea and television, in a house noisy with youngsters.

Monday was an interminable day for Richard. His bruised forehead still ached from the bashing on the kitchen wall. The final chapters of his autobiography seemed fated to interruption. With only half a mind on work, he couldn't concentrate, or feel any real interest in the story.

Restless and preoccupied, expecting Beth to phone, he wandered in and out. He was sorry for her – but more sorry for himself, because he had depended so much on her coming today. To have to do all the chores for the second day was both tedious and annoying. Then he had to clear up the mess in the kitchen.

Sheba was still tired from yesterday's excursion to Lovington, and seemed disinclined to go out when he was ready for their midday exercise in the field at the end of the lane.

'Now don't you start to be awkward!' he told her, irritably.

Back at the cottage, Richard searched the larder for food, without any interest or appetite, and finally decided on a couple of boiled eggs – timing them exactly five minutes on his braille watch. With a fresh pot of coffee, he sat for some time in the kitchen, wondering if the little dog had died, and whether Beth would come tomorrow. She would naturally be upset, for the dog had been her closest companion for several years. If anything like that should happen to Sheba, he would go mad! But it couldn't, unless it happened to both. If a car should hit them, they would both be killed, or badly injured. He shivered with the ghastly thought. This is ridiculous! I'm getting morbid, he told himself, testily, and went out to the wood shed to saw a few logs for the fire.

His head was throbbing, but he wouldn't give up until he had a small pile of logs at his feet. Beth had dragged several broken branches into the shed before Christmas, and had gathered a lot of firewood in the lane during the Autumn. She was always busy on something or other. The garden had been cleared and planted with bulbs and wallflowers in October.

Filling up the log basket, he felt slightly dizzy, and was glad to sink into the armchair when he had finished.

'That's my quota for today!' he told Sheba, and she was relieved from anxiety at last when she saw his feet on the fender, and a cigarette between his lips.

It had been a restless day after a disturbed night. Something was troubling him. Could it be the woman's voice on the telephone? Sheba vividly remembered other occasions, in the past, when a woman's voice on the telephone had upset her master for days.

The clock struck four. Still only four o'clock? What a long day it seemed! Richard was chain smoking now. He missed the cup of tea they always had in the afternoon, but he was too lazy to get up and do it for himself.

Why hadn't Beth telephoned again?

Would she come in the morning?

It was pretty deadly without her.

Switching on the wireless, he was startled by a loud and penetrating voice, discoursing on the habits of snakes! 'My sainted aunt!'

He switched off quickly, and stood up, yawning and stretching.

'Sheba, girl – I should like to walk to the village, and call on Beth. Do you mind?' he asked, with surprising gentleness.

The village was buzzing with life as they approached; the shops still open. Richard stopped the first person they met on the pavement, asking to be directed to Mrs Walker's cottage in the High Street.

A rasping female voice answered him. 'Mrs Walker? Oh, yes, I know it very well. I'll take you there. It's only just a few yards from where we are standing as a matter of fact.'

Richard smiled his thanks, and Sheba followed the woman, on his instructions, with the same reluctance she had shown all day.

'Here we are,' said the woman.

His arm was clutched, and he was guided down a short path to the door.

'Would you like me to wait to see if she's at home? It's no trouble,' the rasping voice persisted, and he could feel a natural curiosity had crept into her genuine desire to help.

'No thanks, I can manage now.'

He lifted his hand to rap on the door.

'Oh, there's a door knocker. I'll do it for you!'

Drat the woman! Why didn't she go away?

The door swung open, as the knocker dropped. Beth must have seen them approaching, for she showed no surprise in her voice and manner. But then, she was always a very controlled sort of person, and the other woman was still hovering.

'Good afternoon, Miss Hale.'

'Oh, good afternoon, Mrs Walker. I've brought you a visitor!' she tittered.

'How nice!' said Beth, sweetly. 'Won't you come in, Mr Seal?'

'Thank you.'

Richard and Sheba stepped inside, and the door closed firmly on Miss Hale.

'That woman!' said Beth, meaningly.

'Beth – your little dog . . . how is she?'

'She died, early this morning. I sat up all night with her.'

'I'm sorry.'

'Thank you.'

He had a sudden overwhelming urge to comfort her, and reached out his hands. She took them gratefully, and they stood there, for a long moment, in the dark passage, with Sheba between them.

'It was good of you to come, Mr Seal.'

'Mr Seal? But this is ridiculous! Can't you call me Richard?'

'If you wish.'

'I most certainly do!' he insisted.

She dropped his hands. Had he upset her?

'Well, we must be getting back,' he said, briskly. 'I just thought I would call in – we were out for a walk, anyway.'

'I am just having tea. Won't you join me? *Please*!' she added, appealingly.

'Well, if you insist,' he grinned, and Sheba followed her into a room smelling faintly of flowers.

A wood fire crackled, and the atmosphere was friendly and cheerful.

'Won't you take off your coat?'

'Thanks.'

Her hands slipped the coat from his shoulders. It was then that she noticed the ugly bruise on his forehead, and gasped, 'What have you done to your head?'

He grinned. 'It's nothing.'

He was very conscious of those hands – hands which had served him for six months without intruding in any way on his privacy. It was so unusual to find hands without the instinct to possess or control.

'Would Sheba like a drink?' she was asking.

'Thank you.'

He found himself in a comfortable chair, with Sheba beside him and a bowl of water – Cindy's bowl? – on the carpet. So she wasn't too houseproud!

'She won't touch it. Will you tell her she may?'

'Drink up, girl!' he told Sheba, and she lapped the water thirstily.

'Does she never touch anything without your permission?'

'Never!'

'Wonderful,' Beth murmured, busy with tea cups. 'The rest of the puppies were collected today, that's why I couldn't come in,' she explained. 'I couldn't really keep them any longer, they were promised weeks ago. It's always the same, I never want to part with them. But it's time they started road training. I do the house training part before they leave, so there shouldn't be any difficulty in that respect.'

'You will miss them.'

'Yes, I shall.'

Her voice was deliberately calm and controlled. She handed him a cup of tea, and pushed a small table alongside the arm of his chair.

'Would you like a ham sandwich?'

'Thank you.'

He found himself listening for a trace of emotion in her voice, but found none. They were sitting here together, quite normally and naturally. He hadn't known quite what to expect when he called on her without any warning. The ham sandwiches were thin and dainty, with a suspicion of mustard, and the tea tasted good in a thin china cup.

'I shall be in tomorrow,' she told him, as she refilled his cup.

'That's good! I've missed you,' he added, truthfully.

Then he told her about their Sunday excursion to Lovington, for she hadn't much to offer in the way of conversation.

But she was a wonderful listener, even better than Sheba, who was inclined to yawn!

'Well, I do congratulate you. I think that's absolutely marvellous!' she said at last, when he came to the end of their adventure.

He knew she was very impressed. He wanted to impress her. He realised now that it was partly for this reason he had attempted it.

To prove his normality to Beth.

She had never shown any sign of pity in all the time he had known her, and he was determined to be spared that crippling and paralysing insult to his intelligence. But what did she feel?

Curiosity burned, of a sudden, and he asked, bluntly, 'Beth, are you sorry for me?'

Her stillness told him she was not as casual as she pretended to be today. And her voice was no longer calm and controlled. With a little tremor she could not disguise, she said, feelingly, 'I admire you, Richard – tremendously.'

His face seemed to glow in the firelight. His eyes, with their dark intensity, seemed to be searching her very soul for the truth. Then he smiled a slow, satisfied smile.

'Thank you, my dear. May I have another cup of tea, and do I smell chocolate cake?'

'You do!' She laughed indulgently, and put a generous slice on his plate.

All his rebelliousness seemed to be absorbed in her gentleness. She sat there so quietly on the other side of the hearth. Yet all the time he was absorbing this extraordinary warmth and affection. It was illuminating and touching. In her company he felt so relaxed his habitual aggressiveness seemed rather absurd and childish. If sensuality had any part in it, then it was so unlike the other as to be unrecognisable. If this was love, why did he feel no wild delight? Was it simply a sweet fulfilment, a long and gradual awakening? 'I admire you, Richard – tremendously.'

Ah, but this time he had to be certain that love was not disguised in pity. He was finished with pretence and the mockery of lies and deception. Beth was balanced. She had no moods, and, unlike Marion, no fear or embarrassment in his blindness.

This, then, was her most endearing trait, that she found him as he found himself – a normal man, without sight.

Again, that faint, elusive scent of flowers. He turned his head, sniffing the air inquiringly.

'Violets,' she said. 'I couldn't resist them in the florist's this morning. I was feeling sad, and they held out a promise of Spring.'

'Your snowdrops are still there, under the old pear tree,' he reminded her, gently.

'They are?' She was pleased he had remembered to look at them.

It was strange, yet natural, to be sitting here together, he thought. Not saying very much, but content.

In retrospect they were almost strangers, reluctant to delve too deeply into closed chapters. Richard felt he had already divulged enough about his early environment and marriage, and he did not intend to burden Beth with any more such reminiscences. Neither did he propose to bombard her with questions, or draw reluctant confessions from her own remote past. They had both matured. Youth, and the follies and mistakes of youth, should be left alone.

He wished now he had never embarked on that autobiography, though he hadn't dug very deeply into his private thoughts. Probing was the birth of possession, and possession the ultimate destruction of human love and understanding. Once he had been foolish enough to believe that a man and a woman should bare their souls to each other. Never again! Only fools made the same mistake twice.

If Beth was reticent, he would respect her reticence, for this strange remoteness was part of her charm. He was never quite sure of her – and that was a good thing, for it kept a man guessing. He smiled and reached for her hand.

'Well, I must be getting back. I've enjoyed this enormously! You have no idea what it means to me to *touch* you. I've been wanting to, you know, for some time, but I didn't dare!' he confessed, with such surprising candour, she laughed, affectionately – but did not disclose she had felt the same way.

Helping him on with his overcoat, she was very conscious of Sheba's disapproval, and it saddened her.

'I should feel so much happier, Richard, if you could make Sheba understand I am not trying to take her place.'

'I will, Beth. Leave it to me!' he promised, boastfully.

But her eyes were clouded with doubt as she watched them walk away, with such proud and purposeful independence. Was there really a permanent place for her in their lives?

The final chapter was reached by the end of April. 'The Sea Was My Mistress' was finished at last!

'Hurray!' – the joyous shout startled Sheba, and brought Beth hurrying in from the kitchen with flour on her hands, and a happy smile on her face.

Richard gripped her shoulders, embraced her exuberantly, and yelled, 'Where's the champagne? We've got to celebrate!'

'Careful, dear, I'm covered in flour,' she reminded him, dropping her bared arms on his own shoulders, where the flour sprinkled the floor, and not his clothes – she was rather proud of that nice green cardigan she had knitted since Christmas!

They were both tall, and her face, on a level with his own, held a new animation, that could almost be described as gay. The change had come about gradually, following weeks of indecision and loneliness, after Cindy's death. But now she had finally made up her mind to let the future take care of itself. She would make no demands on this man. He was like a lion in a cage, some days – fretting to be free, a restless creature, with a pale, tormented face. Only Sheba really understood these black moods. Only Sheba had the selfless devotion to accept everything – to share both the 'glory and the agony'.

But these black days were balanced evenly now with days of such peace and contentment, and Beth could only dread the one and enjoy the other. She expected no miracles in this man, already in his mid-forties, and with such astounding arrogance and self-importance. Not for Richard the 'humble-pie' or 'second fiddle'. He must be the sole administrator of his little world; looking inwards, to his own reflection, rather than outwards, to the reflection of Sheba and Beth. Utterly self-absorbed, he saw them both as his disciples now, and knew, without a shadow of doubt, they would be willing to go through hell with him – if hell was his next objective! But it wasn't – oh, no! He had wonderful plans for the future, but they must wait until Andy got back from Singapore!

'Pack it up, Beth. Get rid of it! I don't want to see it again! You will find the publisher's address in my desk – third pigeonhole from the left,' he added, precisely. 'I leave the marketing entirely to you. If this chap sends it back, try another publisher.'

Then he kissed the tip of her nose in an absent-minded way and demanded – 'Well, aren't you proud of me, Woman?'

'Terribly!'

Her smile was touched with sadness now, for it was the end of a period of definite work and obligation. What would he do next? Where would he go?

The very next day he was off to Ovingdean with Sheba, and

a large suitcase! He had the same exuberance of a young boy going home from boarding school for the holidays.

'It's all organised,' he had shouted upstairs, where she was busy sorting out clean shirts and underwear. 'I've told them I'm coming for a few days – possibly a week, and I've ordered a taxi for nine o'clock. Can you get here a bit earlier to see me off? Why not stay here while I'm away?'

'Why not?' she echoed.

She hadn't anything to hurry back for these days – no little heart beating with excitement as she came up the path – no little face at the window. She still missed Cindy intolerably.

'Yes, I think I will stay here while you are away. It will be a good opportunity to get some cleaning done,' she decided. 'And the garden needs some attention,' she added.

'Good girl,' was Richard's only comment.

Since that day he had called on Beth, their relationship had changed, but neither of them had commented on the change. She had her wages paid monthly now, at the local branch of Barclay's Bank. But when she went to collect it, she found, to her surprise, that the amount had been increased, quite considerably, at Richard's instructions.

Because her own home was so lonely, she was often on her bicycle, en route to Rose Cottage, soon after eight o'clock in the morning, and not returning until late evening.

Afternoon tea was a leisurely, relaxed meal, by the fireside, and Rose Cottage, her second home, seemed reluctant to part with her when dusk was falling over the quiet fields, and Richard taking his last walk of the day with Sheba. She could see them from the kitchen window, pacing the measured track their feet had trod for nearly a year. Tears would gather in her eyes, and her heart ached with love for him as he paced up and down. With the sea in his blood, he was still haunted by the past, still very much a seafaring man. Dear Richard! If only he could go to sea again, in some other capacity? If he could feel the deck under his feet, and the salt spray in his face – would he be happy again – really happy?

She would make no move to hold him if the opportunity came. She would not have him any different. She loved him, in his cruelty and kindness, in his anger and penitence, in his frustration and fulfilment. But her love was not wholly maternal, for often she was disturbed by the force of her emotions, and her racing pulses.

This man, by a touch of his hand, or a glancing look from his sightless face, had more power to excite her than her young husband, all those years ago. Vague longings, for so long dormant, became increasingly demanding. She was alive at last! It was delicious, but dangerous! Yes, it was a good thing he was going away for a few days, for she would have time to practise a little self-control. After all, she was old enough, and intelligent enough, to realise that Richard had finished with one passionate love affair, and had no desire to start another. Besides, he had not even suggested marriage. Was she not being a little premature?

But when the taxi had disappeared round the bend of the lane, and she went back to the empty rooms, so pregnant with his vital personality, she was conscious only of an aching heart, and a tightened throat. They had been shaking hands quite formally at the open window of the taxi, when she had suddenly and impulsively touched his cheek with her lips – and he had turned his face with a sudden jerk, and kissed her mouth. She was still trembling, still trying to decide whether he had intended to kiss her that way or whether he was just being polite! Her cheeks were burning, more from embarrassment than anything else. But then she remembered the tone of his voice, and the expression on his face . . .

'Goodbye, my dear. Take care of yourself. I hope to have some good news for you within a day or so. I'll give you a ring!'

Now what exactly did he mean by that?

Baffled by his unpredictable behaviour, Beth made herself some fresh coffee, and sat down at the kitchen table to review her position.

The possibility of ever being invited to be the second Mrs Seal seemed as remote as ever. For now that she had time to reconsider that last remark of Richard's, she came to the logical conclusion that it had no reference to herself at all. 'Good news' was good news for Richard, and he naturally assumed she would be pleased! It was just unfortunate that she had lost her head, and imagined the words to have a more personal implication.

The truth still stared her in the face. Richard was, and always would be, completely self-absorbed. It was no new and shattering discovery, yet it left her feeling limp and weak with disappointment. In all these months, she had not yet succeeded in balancing her sensitivity to his realism. She had been unconsciously searching for that spark of love the other woman had kindled, and abandoned – but it was not hers to find, she reminded herself reproachfully. She must make up her mind to be satisfied with the crumbs. He had lost faith in human nature. Still tasting the bitter dregs of the divorce, and embittered by this unhappy experience, he was suspicious of every woman. The paradox of his split personality was both frightening and wonderful, and the hard core of truth she had to face seemed bleak and forlorn on this, the first morning without him.

He had taken too much of her spirit already, for she hadn't the strength of mind or will to resist him. Now that he had gone, she sat alone, feeling wretchedly undecided and miserable.

This, then, was her future if she stayed with him.

Shifting her gaze from the open fields to his white cooking apron on the kitchen door – to his muddy boots beside the boiler – to the silent typewriter on his desk in the next room – she saw in all these mundane things the man she loved, with his indomitable courage and determination. Cooking, gardening, typing – he was so incredibly versatile!

She hadn't to search her heart for the answer, for she knew already what the answer would be. If he wanted her, she would stay. It was as simple as that, and no amount of reasoning would make it any different.

The breakfast dishes had not been washed, dead ashes strewed the hearth, an unmade bed and scattered clothes littered the bedroom, and the morning post had brought several letters. But she discarded it all quite casually, and wandered out to the garden.

She had all day – two, three, four days, possibly a week, to clean and polish, to wash and iron, and get up to date with the correspondence. Richard's manuscript must be packed and posted to the publisher. But all this could wait. Loneliness and heartache dwelt only in these empty rooms.

In the garden it was Spring again, and daffodils were growing where the snowdrops had been. All of nature was there to remind her of the miracle within the scope of her *seeing* eyes. She stood there, silent and thoughtful, closing her eyes to the sunlight, to the green, budding lilacs, the bright yellow daffodils, the trees and the fields. This was Richard's world – this Springtime of his sightless year, in which he had but the elements to remind him of passing seasons. Wind and rain and sun, but no colour, no light, no shape or beauty of leaf and flower.

'If I were blind, and had no calendar, what would the seasons mean to me?' she thought. 'I should recognise Spring in the faint scent of the primrose, and the song of the blackbird – Summer with roses, and new-mown hay – Autumn with bonfires and roasting chestnuts – Winter with frosted finger-tips, and rain on my face. But what did the seasons mean to Richard? Surely not the same earthy, elementary things? Perhaps he measured them in terms of sport? – cricket, rugger, rowing, swimming, athletics, tobogganing. All these had played an important part in his young life, for she had seen the album of photographs in the drawer in the bedroom – and wept over them.

Leaning against the south wall of the cottage, with the warm sun on her lifted face, Beth kept her eyes closed. By doing so, she could see all her imagined grievances and disappointments, in the light of Richard's sightless eyes.

And they were very insignificant!

Of course he looked inward!

Where else could he look?

Self was so important because it was the only reality – the only substantial evidence of continuity and purpose.

She opened her eyes with a tremendous sense of gratitude, to look once more on the bright, yellow daffodils, the green, budding lilac, the trees and the fields.

Then she went in search of a spade, and began to dig, in happy and absorbed contentment.

9

Andy McLaren, back from the Far East, was waiting at Ovingdean to greet Richard on arrival.

In civilian dress, short, balding and inclined to stoutness, he was still unassuming. But he was a very likeable person, and a loyal friend – the only loyal friend of that seafaring era – Richard could depend upon. The bond between them was closer than ever, in spite of frequent partings, and Andy's long absences.

He had booked in at his usual hotel at Rottingdean, and, as always, made St Dunstan's at Ovingdean their rendezvous.

Richard had phoned the hotel one evening, ascertained that a Mr McLaren had already arrived but was out, and left a message. He knew he could count on Andy to be waiting at Ovingdean, and he was not disappointed.

As he stepped out of the taxi with Sheba, a familiar voice, with its unmistakable inflection, hailed him from a front window.

'Hullo there! Hold on for a wee second now, and I'll be with you!'

Then his hand was being pumped exuberantly, and an arm flung over his shoulders.

'Richard! – it's grand to see you. Why, man, you look marvellous! And Sheba, as beautiful as ever!'

Sheba regarded him with calm and friendly composure. She had no fear of this particular person. He could be trusted, so she allowed herself to be fondled, and even her chin to be tickled, with most unusual docility!

'Andy! Why, you old Son-of-a-Gun! Where have you been hiding yourself?'

It was always the same sort of greeting. It hadn't changed in twenty years. Andy picked up the suitcase, linked his arm in Richard's, and asked, provocatively, 'Well, how's the new housekeeper?'

Richard grinned.

'I'm not sure I'm going to tell you. You might want to collar her for yourself!'

'Oh, come on – be a sport!'

'Well, let's have a drink, and I'll think about it. But first, I have to present myself to the Commandant and Matron, and find my room. You'd better come along with me.'

'You bet I will. I'm no letting you out of my sight! How long are you staying?'

'That depends on you. How long can you stay?'

'A week to ten days.'

'That's fine, then I'll do the same. I love the feel of this place, Andy. It's like a second home to me,' Richard confessed, as he walked easily and effortlessly to the Commandant's office.

He was familiar with every part of the house and grounds, and had no hesitation in going to the beach by way of the tunnel under the road, whenever he felt like it. He was leading Andy now, and it was Andy who felt an outsider. From all directions they were greeted by strong, cheerful voices as Richard's own voice, raised in excitement, penetrated the rooms they were passing. The Commandant's welcome was equally enthusiastic.

'Ah, here comes our conquering hero!' was his greeting. 'Why, you look like a million dollars. What have you been up to since Christmas?'

'He's got a lovely housekeeper! That might have something to do with it!' Andy suggested, mildly.

'Poor Richard! Spare his blushes!'

And they all laughed.

'Well, Matron is dying to see you, as usual; you were always one of her favourites!' the pleasant voice reminded Richard.

'He tells everyone that!' muttered Richard, as they went in search of Matron.

They found her in a small ante-room filling vases with Spring flowers. The scent of narcissi pervaded the room. She smiled at the tall, handsome figure, and the striking-looking dog – laid a spray of mimosa carefully on the bench, and held out both hands in greeting.

'Hullo, Richard. It's lovely to see you!'

She took his hands, and kissed his cheek, affectionately.

'It's my privilege to kiss all my old boys!' she reminded Andy – whose face, at Ovingdean, was almost as familiar as Richard's.

A telephone call interrupted their friendly chat, and she hurried away, with a reminder that she would expect to see them after supper. They would join her for coffee. Richard was allocated one of the bedrooms reserved for visiting 'old boys' and he knew exactly where to find it.

To Andy's undisguised amusement, he led the way with easy self-assurance. Then he unpacked his case, and carefully arranged everything in its proper place, without any fumbling or hesitation. Although Andy had seen it happen so many times in the past, he could never take it for granted.

After all these years, he was still astounded, still admiring – and still reminding himself that he was responsible. He hadn't dare mention it to Richard again, for when he had confessed to being five minutes late on watch that fateful night, and consequently Richard was still on the bridge, he had been told to shut up, and not to talk such utter drivel! But the sense of guilt was still with him, and revived every time they met. His were the eyes that should have been blinded – not Richard's.

Andy stood there, at the open window, watching those deft, unflurried hands, smoothing a suit on its hanger, and filling a drawer with shirts and underwear. Richard's clothes had never looked more immaculate. His shirts and underwear were beautifully laundered. Yes, he really looked cared for now. That housekeeper certainly knew her job. Six clean shirts! But Richard had always been extravagant with shirts, and extremely fastidious about his appearance.

When Andy turned his face away to look across the garden at the sparkling sea, his eyes were damp and his mouth trembling with the old intolerable heartache.

Satisfied that everything was in its proper place, Richard joined him at the open window with a radiant smile on his face. They stood there, with their arms flung lightly over each other's shoulders, and Richard's sightless eyes seemed to be searching the far horizon, with the old, dark gleam.

Sheba stood between them.

'It smells good!' said Richard.

Andy, tight-lipped, said nothing.

'Well, old chap, you've arrived at last – Master of your own ship! You got my cablegram of congratulation?'

'Yes, thanks.'

'Captain of the good ship *Hebrides*!' chuckled Richard, and squeezed Andy's shoulder, affectionately. Then, still straining his eyes to the horizon, he asked, with pretended casualness, 'Does your Purser need a clerk, by any chance?'

For a moment Andy was too stunned to answer. Then his face shone with eagerness.

'Good God, man! Why have I no thought of it before?' he shouted. 'With your clerical training, typing and braille shorthand – you could do it! Aye, you could do it! Purser's clerk?'

He choked on the thought. At last the chance to repay that old debt; a reprieve, perhaps, from that tormenting nightmare he had lived with for twenty years!

Richard's hand was trembling on his arm.

'You – you don't think it's crazy? Andy, tell me the truth.'

'It's no so damn crazy as writing a book!'

They both laughed.

'Oh, that – it's finished and forgotten. Just a hunch I had to get out of my system. I've left it to Beth to find a publisher,' said Richard, lightly.

'Beth, eh? A nice, old-fashioned name,' mused Andy.

'A nice old-fashioned woman!' Richard retorted. Then promptly forgot her.

'How soon can you let me know . . . about this vacancy?'

'I'll make a vacancy, dinna worry. I've a wee bit of influence, and man, I'm going to exert it for once! Leave it to me, it's practically settled!'

Richard was amazed. He had never heard this note of authority in Andy's voice before. He had always seemed so casual, as though he couldn't be bothered. But, of course, he was Master of the *Hebrides* now, and that would account for it.

'Shipmates again!' Andy was saying, recklessly.

Richard turned his face from the distant horizon. He was very pale, his cheeks were wet and his mouth twitching.

'I'm ruddy well crying!' he sobbed.

And Sheba, troubled and confused by the sudden turn of events, barked anxiously.

'It's all right, old girl, you're coming with us. We might even sign you on as the ship's mascot!' Andy reminded her gaily.

'It's time for her supper,' said Richard, consulting his braille watch.

He had a tin of dog meat in his luggage, and Sheba's special bowls. One he filled with water from the tap over the wash-basin, and the other with food. When she was satisfied, they followed her out of the room.

After a quick drink, they both had the same thought – to get down to the beach as soon as possible. Away from the distracting voices, they could talk at length of this wonderful new plan for the future.

The tide was out. As their feet touched the shingle, Richard released Sheba from the white harness, and she streaked across the sand like a greyhound, touched the water with a hesitant paw and streaked back, panting and breathless, to run in circles round them, in great agitation.

'What's the matter with her?' Andy demanded.

'She's fussing like an old hen because she thinks we are going for a swim!' laughed Richard.

Then he told her to stop fussing, and enjoy herself, for they were only taking a walk. He swung the white harness in his hand.

'Don't you understand – you are off duty? Silly girl – be off with you!'

Still a little puzzled and anxious, Sheba trotted away obediently, but kept a wary eye on them as they strode happily along the beach.

Richard walked with the jaunty air of a man with a purpose – his shoulders squared, his arms swinging. His head was lifted proudly, his face illuminated with joy and hope.

'I can't believe it! I can't believe it!' he repeated, with a kind of wonder. 'Andy – my dear chap – you did say it was practically settled, didn't you?'

'I did,' Andy agreed. 'I shall phone the office in the morning. I think I can get young Johnson transferred from the *Hebrides* to the *Balmoral*; she's on the South Africa run now, you know. Johnson's got a girl friend in Cape Town, so that should please him!'

Richard heaved a great sigh of happiness.

'I've had it on my mind to ask you for some time, but I

thought you might raise a few objections. It's quite taken the wind out of my sails that you actually agree to give me a trial. When I heard you had been promoted, I decided it was now or never – nobody, but yourself, could get me back on board as a member of the crew. Even if I had the money, I don't want to travel as a passenger, Andy. I should be bored to tears in a couple of days. But to *work my passage*! My God! Can you understand what that means – after twenty years ashore?'

Andy made no comment.

He was still reminding himself that he could see his way clear at last to remove the stigma of guilt from his conscience. Richard went on talking, and the strong, vibrating voice followed Sheba across the sands. When he had finished, Andy remarked, laconically, 'By the way, our next trip takes us to Montreal.'

'Montreal?' gasped Richard, excitedly. 'An Atlantic crossing? What a tremendous bit of luck!'

'Aye, I thought that would appeal to you. We sail about the middle of next month. When does the lease of your cottage expire?'

'June – but I can get rid of it any time. The rent is paid.'

'What are you proposing to do about your nice housekeeper?'

'Marry her! – if she'll have me.'

Andy choked.

'*Marry* her? Are you crazy? You've just landed yourself a job as a Purser's clerk, and you're practically on your way to Montreal, and you calmly talk of getting married! That sounds to me just a wee bit daft,' he added, dubiously.

'Yes, I was afraid you would see it that way, old chap, after the other affair,' said Richard, with a sigh.

'Does she know how you feel about her?'

'I don't think so.'

'Are you in love with her?'

'I'm not sure. I can't bear the thought of losing her.'

'Yet you want your freedom and independence?'

'I want both – I'm a selfish brute. Beth wouldn't hinder me she would encourage me.'

'She must be an exceptionally understanding person.'

'She's an angel!'

Andy whistled. 'Aye, you love her all right.'

But he was still unconvinced. It was such a risk; the first marriage had been a disaster for both. He thought Richard was making a very serious mistake.

'I've often wondered why you never married, Andy, with all the women you've met. Was there a reason?' asked Richard, with sudden interest.

'I have'na given it much thought lately,' said Andy, with a chuckle. 'I guess I'm the confirmed bachelor. There was a girl I should have liked to know better, but when I got around to making inquiries after the war, she was already married!'

'That was rotten luck.'

'Not at all, sheer laziness on my part. But it all happened a long time ago – twenty years, in fact.'

'Twenty years? Anybody I knew?'

'As a matter of fact, you did, but only slightly. You were rather exalted in those days, my friend!'

Richard grinned, quite unabashed.

'Who was she?'

'Elizabeth Davies.'

'Good Lord! I had no idea.'

'Of course you hadn't. As Acting Second Officer, you were far too superior to mix with the lower orders!' jeered Andy.

'Lower orders, my foot! – and you a University chap. Don't talk such rot! As for Liz, well, she was no ordinary stewardess. I remember wondering why she had chosen such a life.'

'Her father was a Commodore in the First World War. Didn't you know? Liz was very nautically minded, but a bad sailor, unfortunately.'

'Then why didn't she join the Wrens and get a job ashore?'

'She applied – passed the oral examination, but failed the medical. So she volunteered as a stewardess on the *Braemar* for the duration of the war. Poor Liz, that did'na last long either.'

'You seem to know a hell of a lot about our Liz.'

'Aye, I had a hell of a lot of time being disgustingly sick – and so did Liz!'

'Yes, I remember now. But why didn't you get around to making a proper date with her – ashore, I mean?'

'We had no time,' said Andy, quietly. 'I have no set eyes on Liz since that day the old *Braemar* was sunk. But her name was on the list of survivors. Besides, she would'na look twice at me, with you around – you great big Casanova!'

'But that's ridiculous – I hardly knew the girl!'

'She was in love with you,' Andy declared stubbornly.

They walked on in silence, for both had their memories of the old *Braemar* and that ghastly night which had altered the pattern of their lives.

Andy changed the subject abruptly. 'You must be starving. When did you last have a meal?'

'Beth gave me sandwiches and an apple to eat on the train, and I got a cup of coffee from somebody's flask. I'm usually pretty lucky when I travel.'

'But that was hours ago. Come on, let's turn back now, and we should be just in time for supper.'

'You're the boss, Captain McLaren!' grinned Richard, whistling for Sheba.

Dismissing from his mind for ever all the horrors of that night in mid-Atlantic, he faced the future with complete confidence. He would give Beth a ring after supper, and tell her the wonderful news of his new appointment, and ask her to get the spare bedroom ready. If Andy had ten days' leave, then he may as well spend part of it at the cottage.

Then he could meet Beth.

Hoots of laughter greeted their breathless entry into the dining room, as the soup was being served.

'Come on you two – late again!'

It was almost like being back at boarding school, but not quite so dignified.

They were not compelled to attend chapel on Sunday morning, indeed, there was little compulsion at Ovingdean. But it seemed the correct thing to do, and it pleased both Matron and the Commandant. For this reason, alone, Richard had always felt a little guilty when he excused himself, and quite justifiably pious when he attended without being prompted. Whenever Andy stayed at Rottingdean over the weekend, he always walked over to Ovingdean on Sunday morning. For Andy, there was no compulsion either, but a sense of duty and reverence for the Lord's Day, firmly established as a child with strictly Presbyterian parents, had followed him through manhood.

Sunday morning service on board ship, conducted by the ship's Captain, was strictly observed. It was one of the laws of the Medes and Persians that all the ship's officers should attend. After attending hundreds of such services, Andy stood, at last, in the shoes of 'the old man' and acknowledged it a great privilege, for he attached a lot of importance to this short and simple illustration of their firm belief in the Almighty. In Andy's opinion, no seafaring man could be other than God-fearing. From the moment they 'cast off' till they 'tied up' again, they were literally in the hands of God. Whether they travelled east or west, north or south, they were still at the mercy of the elements – and the elements were God, in all His power and glory.

'I believe in God' they repeated, like parrots, Sunday after Sunday, but you had to recognise the profound truth of that statement or it was just so much repetition, and a mockery, without any fundamental meaning.

'Eternal Father, strong to save' – the favourite hymn of all who 'went down to the sea in ships' – how many times had he joined in the singing in his twenty years? Andy had lost count – it must be hundreds, but the words and the tune had an eternity for Andy. Anyone who had sung that hymn in a howling Atlantic gale would know what he meant – an overwhelming conviction of this Eternity, and the God who rules the winds and the waves.

So when Andy turned up punctually for chapel at Ovingdean that Sunday morning, Richard was not at all surprised.

He enjoyed the sense of interest and admiration which accompanied them wherever they went – and so did Sheba! As Andy so coarsely indicated, 'they lapped it up'. Most of the time they were putting on an act for the benefit of their public.

It had become an obligation.

In the beginning of their relationship, this 'showing off' had been a mixture of funk and defiance. They had to be expert navigators, or they would be parted, for ever.

The thought was intolerable.

It never happened, but the fear and the possibility were there.

So they adopted this supreme self-confidence, which in turn became arrogance. The majority of people admired it, some thought it was 'over done', and a small minority simply did not notice.

Andy, of course, was one of the majority. He always followed Richard and Sheba, never led. His early admiration and hero-worship had stayed with him through the years. When he said to himself – 'I would die for that man' – he really meant it.

So he followed them into the Chapel, to thank God, not

only for his own sight, but for this wonderful opportunity to sail together again – and to repay the debt he had been owing for half a lifetime. Uplifted by these thoughts, he knelt to pray with new earnestness and dedication.

Richard's elbow touched his own. Sheba, hearing the traffic of feet and the unaccustomed tapping of white sticks, turned her head to look at her master, on his knees in the crowded pew, with his hands over his face. Tentatively, she reached out a paw to touch his arm, but it was quickly and definitely put back. He did not want sympathy then? She must wait until he did. Her limpid eyes followed his every movement, and when he finally sat up and turned his face towards her, she was surprised and overjoyed by its expression. A hand reached down and tweaked her ear.

She shivered in a great surge of love for him which seemed to hold a new and strange significance. She felt a presentiment of some impending event – not trouble! This would be disturbing to their present circumstances perhaps, and she might have to learn new ideas and fresh routes? It had happened before, and it would happen again, for he was a restless, unpredictable creature! But she could see in his enraptured face, and in the vibration which passed between them, that it would bring him happiness. This other man, who was a friend, had always brought a sense of goodwill and comradeship.

Now Richard was singing!

He was singing with tremendous enthusiasm, as he sang in his bath! Sheba was satisfied. Richard was singing with such unusual gusto, heads were turning, and members of the staff smiled to each other. Several of the senior staff, remembering him in all stages of his development from the very beginning of his long association with St Dunstan's, felt a warm glow of personal pride and satisfaction.

For he *was* outstanding, but had to be admired and respected rather than loved. They remembered his devastation when the broken marriage was finally dissolved. He had been defeated by the forces of his own rebellious nature, rather than the fickleness of a young and beautiful woman. They had been sorry for both, knowing how difficult Richard could be.

But he went away alone, like a stricken animal, to lick his wounds in private, they remembered. There was something elemental and primitive in much of his behaviour, which found its match in the huge, powerful dog, who was his constant companion. But now that dark, shadowed face was once again vividly alive and alight with some new, exciting discovery, or adventure!

He could not hide his excitement. It flowed from every part of him with undisguised frankness!

The lesson, taken from the forty-second chapter of Isaiah, was a great favourite at Ovingdean. It was noticed that Richard's rapt face was absorbing every word that morning. They were right. The words had a new significance – a personal significance for Richard, that day.

Wonderful words!

Sing unto the Lord a new song and his praise from the end of the earth, ye that go down to the sea . . . And I will bring the blind by a way that they knew not; I will lead them in paths that they have not known; I will make darkness light before them, and crooked things straight. These things will I do unto them, and not forsake them . . .

If you believed that, then there was no obstacle to the blind man's search for equality and recognition. No mountain too high, no river too wide – no limit to his capacity.

If you believed it?

But he did!

Surely, by believing in himself, he could climb the highest mountain – and meet God, halfway?

Beth could hear Richard talking excitedly as they came in the gate, then the three figures darkened the doorway, and he called out jocularly.

'Where's that charming housekeeper of mine? Come and be introduced.'

'Here I am,' she said, her heart thudding with pleasure at the sound of his voice. She took his outstretched hand, and he squeezed it affectionately. The arm he flung over her shoulder was a little embarrassing in front of a stranger. A stranger? She was blushing like a schoolgirl now.

'Well, here she is, Andy. You've heard enough about her in the past few days, you hardly need an introduction. This is Beth, and I don't have to tell you, Beth, who this is – none other than the delectable Andy McLaren, and the only chap to put up with my foul temper for the past twenty odd years!'

Richard's face was radiant. She had never seen him so positively happy and excited. Over Sheba's head she clasped the firm strong hand of the man who was regarding her with a puzzled expression.

'Surely no two women in my life could look at me with those same kind brown eyes?' Andy was thinking. But the grey head and the name? If this was the Liz of the old *Braemar*, then that deep blush was something else she had kept from those early days of their acquaintance.

Richard was turning his head from one to the other, and his keen intelligent face was the face of that young naval officer on the bridge. His was the figure at the masthead; his the undisputed lead in this unrehearsed drama.

So they waited, these three, and the faithful Sheba was as much a part in the drama as Andy and Beth. They waited for the astonishing news he was dying to tell; and if Andy was already familiar with it he kept silent, for this was Richard's 'finest hour', that had no equal.

'Are you listening, Beth?' he began. 'It's happened just as I dreamed! Can you believe it? I've got a posting to the *Hebrides* – Andy's *Hebrides*, for he's the Master. I'm to work my passage as a Purser's clerk, and Sheba is coming with me; we sail for Montreal next month!' His sightless eyes had never been so bright and black – black as an onyx in his pale quivering face.

'Congratulations, Richard, I'm so happy for you,' Beth spoke quietly, and her own eyes were wet. She knew it was the end of a chapter for her, that Richard might not ever need her again as he had in the past year, with such desperate urgency. Back where he rightly belonged, in his man's world, it would be Andy's turn to keep an eye on him – this dauntless creature they both loved so dearly. She wondered how long it would be before Andy recognised her. Surely she must have changed out of all recognition? Apart from a lot of extra weight, and thinning hair, Andy looked much the same.

'Where's the sherry?' Richard was demanding impatiently. And when she had filled the glasses, they drank to the future of the new Purser's clerk, while Sheba lapped thirstily from her bowl of cold water.

'Now a second toast!' Richard declared boisterously. 'Come here, Beth, my dear, and give me your hand. Andy, fill the glasses!' They did as he bid, for they both could guess the reason for this second toast.

'To us!' He kissed Beth's cheek, with boyish enthusiasm. He hadn't meant to be unkind, or to make their engagement seem of such little importance, compared to the other. It was just his way. And Beth seemed not to mind about being his fourth love – for the sea was his first love, then there was Marion, and Sheba. Catching her eye, Andy's lips moved soundlessly on the one questioning word 'Liz?' She nodded and smiled.

'Now it's my turn for a toast,' he said, returning the smile with the old friendliness. 'To the three shipmates from the old *Braemar* – Richard, Andy and Liz.'

'Liz?' echoed Richard in frowning disbelief.

'The same,' Andy confirmed.

'Beth, is this true?' Richard's listening face was strained and searching.

'I'm afraid so,' she confessed, in a small choked voice.

'Aye, and you're a darned lucky fellow,' said Andy. 'If I had'na been so lazy, our Liz could have been Mrs Andy McLaren twenty years ago!'

'Do you really think so, old chap?' said Richard, with a smile of disarming sweetness.